TRICKSTER

Tom Moorhouse

OXFORD
UNIVERSITY PRESS

PROLOGUE

There are countless rat stories, but always the most precious are of names. For when rats meet the Taker on a brightmoon raid, or huddled, dim-eyed, beneath the earth, they bear him their name as proof of their worth. And what becomes of the nameless, who have nothing but flesh, fur, and whiskers, no rat knows. In some stories their bones litter the floor of the Taker's burrow, while in others they are born again, to live until their name is earned—and only then can they pass through the Land of Bones.

But the Greenhedge rats speak differently of such things. They have seen what a rat will do to gain a name. And the oldest among them once knew the Shining One, and his tainted brother. Which of those rats, they ask, would the Taker refuse? Which lived without honouring their name? And they mutter that names can be more tricksy than you know.

The ratlings too have stories of that time, though they were not yet born. They tell of two rats who shared a name, who ran with the Taker himself and paid the price. The oldest rats, who know the truth, do not no-say them, for they know that a tale will grow tall if it is any tale at all. But if a ratling asks about names, and if the mood takes them, the old-ones might smile and lower their voices. And then they will tell the oldest tale, the end of which every rat knows by heart:

And so love the Mother, run with the Hunter, and dance with the Trickster. But keep a place, deep and safe, and fill it with your name. For one day you will meet the Taker in his Land of Bones. And it is best to be ready.

Chapter one

'Gabble.'

'Gabble!'

'Gabble, wake up.'

Gentle paws shook at Gabble's shoulders. He came awake in the homely gloom of the family burrow. No light ever reached this deep, but the quiet of the clan told him that it was early, that night had not yet come.

'Mothers?'

They did not answer, intent on rummaging in the dried grasses around him. He frowned and drew down their scent. It was almost the same as ever, as warm and familiar as the earth walls around him. But now it was laced with their concerns; Whisker's resignation and Bustle's worry. The rummaging stopped and Whisker straightened.

'You're right, he's gone,' she said. 'Drat the rat, we just missed him.'

Gone? Gabble felt the chill at his side, the space in the nest where his brother should be. He groaned. *Oh no. Not Ash. Not again.*

'Right, my boy,' said Whisker to Gabble. 'Where is he this time?'

'I don't know,' said Gabble. 'Sorry.'

'It's a name raid tonight,' said Bustle, fretfully. 'You know what he's like.'

Yes, he knew what Ash was like. And if it was a name raid, and Ash was missing, there was only one place he would be found: right where he shouldn't be, where the Mothers couldn't go after him. Gabble staggered to his feet, brushing away the grasses that clung to him. 'I'll go and fetch him.'

'I think you should,' said Whisker. 'Especially after last time.'

Gabble swallowed. Last time had not been fun. He took a step towards the tunnel, but Bustle stopped him, paws on his fur. Her whiskers tickled as she lowered her head to his. 'Gabble, we know it's hard for him. We do.' She spoke quickly, anxiously. 'But he has to wait. He must, especially now you're so nearly ratlings, and our scent won't protect you . . .' She cleared her throat. 'Look after him for us. Promise you will.'

Gabble placed his paw on the soft fur of her shoulder. 'I'll try, Mother.'

'Use your words,' she added. 'He listens to you.'

'Heh,' said Gabble. 'Not often, I think.'

'No, but still more than he listens to us,' said Whisker, drily. She led Bustle gently aside and turned to Gabble. 'Your brother is a rat born without sense, and despite our best efforts he's still a twit.' She sighed. 'Just try to stop him doing anything too stupid, eh?'

'I'll look after him. I promise.'

'Good,' said Whisker. 'Well, get on with you, then.'

And Gabble dashed from the nest, scampering up the tunnel to the common grounds. The walls lightened as he raced, revealing scuffs, roots, and claw-marks, and with the rising light came the ever-present clan chatter. A manic jumble of whistles, cries, squabbles, and chuckles echoed up from the tunnels and swirled around Gabble as he pitched out onto the hard earth of the high places, the common grounds. Scents assailed him: Bigrats, uncles, mothers, ratlings, flapfeet, and pups, all mingled but still distinct. But Gabble had no time for these. He was seeking the only rat who counted. He picked up a tendril of Ash's scent and ran, following as it twisted through the colony.

'Watch it, flapfoot!'

A group of ratlings barged into him, then past, laughing and jostling. Gabble barely spared them a glance but ran on. There was no mistaking Ash's path now. Turn after turn led upward, to the raid chamber. Tunnels and branches tore past as Gabble weaved up, up through the fabric of the colony, making for the highest chamber of all. A curve, a bend, a corner—and daylight stung his eyes, bringing him to a halt.

He hesitated, one foot raised and breath coming fast. Two more steps would take him beyond where any flapfoot was allowed. They would take him into the raid chamber itself—on the night of a raid, when any who were not ratlings or Bigrats were forbidden. A breeze billowed in, cutting fresh through the burrow fug. But even so, the scent of old raids was overwhelming. Acrid and musky, it sent a slow thrum of blood pulsing to Gabble's paws. He should not be here. Not this close to duskfall. He should stay away, out of respect for the Hunter, and for the raiders. But Ash's scent was strong, and from around the bend came the scamper of paws on earth, and a rat making enthusiastic 'Hah' noises. Gabble's jaw set. Oh yes, Ash was in there all right.

Gabble glanced longingly back at the darkness behind him. He wished he were almost anywhere else. He wished he had a normal brother. But he wasn't and didn't. And there was nothing else for him to do. So he raised his muzzle and walked around the corner, narrowing his eyes as he stepped over the threshold.

Sunlight, low and red, flooded the chamber. It bathed some walls crimson but left others in shadow, all the deeper for its nearness to the light. And between the dark and the light ran Ash, now investigating a patch of fallen earth, now scenting at the air. He raced here and there in a frenzy of investigation, his eyes sparkling. The light cast his fur in different colours, frost-white in the shade, red in the dusklight, and black as he crossed the entrance.

Gabble watched Ash's enthusiastic antics from the tunnel mouth and sighed. *Why me?* Then he raised his voice. 'Whatzit, Ash,' he called, softly.

Ash, up on his haunches and paws on the wall, froze. Then he twisted around and his face split into a grin. 'Ah, whatzit, Gabbley! So you came. That's good.' He dropped down and bounded over to where Gabble stood. 'Are you going to raid with me?'

Gabbley. Heh. Ash knew he hated being called that, but did it anyway because he thought it was funny. Ash thought lots of things were funny that weren't. Gabble shook his head. 'Heh. I don't think so. We're not meant to be here.'

Ash's enthusiasm was undiminished. '*I* am. I'm going raiding.'

11

'You remember last time?'

The grin fell from Ash's face. 'It won't be like last time.' He turned to gaze out at the twilight. 'This time I'll do it.'

'They won't let you, I think. You're a flapfoot.' He gestured at Ash's flank. 'And you're not marked.'

Ash's smile returned. He waved a paw, dismissively. 'Ack, that doesn't matter.'

But Ash knew better than anyone that it *did* matter. If you weren't marked with 'respect' by the other ratlings you would die a drudge before you could raid. Or, in Ash's case, you would be dragged home to the Mothers—scuffed and battered but still defiant—by a furious Bigrat.

Gabble glanced nervously at the tunnel. 'Stop mucking around and let's get out of here.'

'You go. I'm raiding.' Ash laughed at Gabble's expression. 'Look, I have a plan, OK? All I need is one ratling to mark me.'

Gabble stared. 'You have head problems, I think. None of them are going to—'

He broke off as large ratling pattered out of the tunnel and stopped dead at the sight of them. Gabble knew him: Hector, a decent sort who didn't give the younger rats a hard time. But now Hector was gazing from Gabble to Ash, a deepening scowl on his face.

Gabble started talking. 'We're really sorry. Heh. We're not here. Well, we are, but we won't be soon. We're just going, aren't we, Ash?' Gabble made a grab for his brother, but Ash skipped out of reach.

'Not me, Gabbley.' He winked at Hector. 'I'm going raiding.'

Hector's ears went flat with outrage. The tunnel behind him echoed with scurrying, and more ratlings entered, filling the air with their odour. Gabble could smell their marks of respect, freshly granted. He burned with the urge to be anywhere else. A female, Groom, from a neighbouring burrow, shoved forwards.

'Flapfeet,' she said, disgusted. 'What are they doing here?'

Hector nodded at Ash. 'I know this one. He's the white rat. The one that causes the problems.'

And Ash's expression went hard. He put his head on one side and pattered forwards a step. He met Hector's gaze with a challenging stare. Gabble held his breath. The ratlings' favourite game was to tumble cheeky flapfeet and send them packing. But to Gabble's surprise Hector merely sighed.

'I don't want your trouble, flapfoot. Not before my name raid,' he said. He stepped aside. 'Go now, and we'll forget this.'

The other raiders exchanged glances but eased apart, opening a path back down to the burrow. No tunnel in Gabble's entire life had ever looked more inviting.

'Ash,' he hissed, 'we need to go. Now.'

But Ash whirled to face him with a flash of anger. 'No. I told you. I'm going to raid.'

'But why?' Gabble was almost pleading. 'We'll be ratlings soon enough. Why not wait, heh? Then we can raid together.' He opened his paws. 'Please? For me?'

Ash's eyes widened, and he half lifted a paw. 'Gabble, I—'

'He's right, flapfoot,' said Hector, cutting him short. 'You should wait. You're too small to dance with the Taker. You will be dishonoured.'

Ash's eyes glittered as he stepped up, nose to nose with Hector.

'You think I fear to meet the Taker? You think I'd dishonour the raid?' Ash's voice was low, and held a strange, hard note. His frame seemed bigger, somehow, shining white. 'Well, you're wrong. I'm not afraid.' An odd smile twitched in Ash's whiskers and he blinked his red eyes. 'Can you say the same?' He fixed Hector, then each ratling in turn with his stare. He drew down their scents. 'Oh, I can smell you. You *do* fear his Land of Bones.'

And Hector could not meet Ash's eyes. The other ratlings shuffled uncomfortably.

'Thought so,' said Ash, quietly. 'But don't worry, he won't take you tonight.' He paused, still with that smile on his lips. 'Because he won't want to meet a bunch of uglies like you any sooner than he has to.'

Ash burst out laughing, scampering backwards. Hector's face darkened and he sidled forwards, teeth bared. Gabble quickly stepped in front of him.

'Hector, please, you shouldn't, he's only—'

But Hector thrust him aside and lashed out, pummelling at Ash's flank. It was over in an instant, Hector turning coldly away, and Ash staggering back, face livid with excitement and triumph. Gabble ran to his brother and scented his flank. Where Hector's paws had touched Ash two smudges of scent clung to his coat. Gabble went cold.

'There,' rasped Hector. 'If you want to raid then there's your "respect". I hope it gives you what you want.'

Ash smiled, all trace of his anger gone. 'Oh, it has,' he said, happily. 'See, Gabble? Hector made me a raider!'

A mutter rose from among the ratlings. Hector crouched, tail writhing. Gabble braced, ready for more trouble. But then the chamber fell silent around them. The ratlings at the rear scurried aside to reveal an uncle, shouldering his way through. Hector spotted him and quickly straightened. But not before he had attracted the other's frown.

'Name raiding,' said the uncle, coming to a halt in the centre of the chamber, 'is no time for ratling play, Hector.'

'No, Uncle,' said Hector. 'Sorry.'

The uncle nodded, then ran his eye over the assembled rats. 'My name is Grist,' he intoned. 'But my true name is Ro'nar. It means "Bold One", and I earned it in the raid. You, who tonight I guide, may know this.' At the mention of his true name the ratlings went utterly still. A true name was a rat's dearest gift, never to be carelessly spoken. 'I am a Bigrat of the Greenhedge,' Grist continued, 'and I bring the Hunter's blessing to your raid.' Grist's eye settled on Gabble and Ash and his frown deepened. 'And you're raiding, are you?'

'No,' said Gabble, quickly.

But Ash nodded. 'That's right.'

Grist regarded them for some moments. Then he bent down and scented Ash's flank. He grunted. 'You are small to name raid. You haven't grown into your feet.'

'Yes, Uncle,' said Gabble. 'We're not yet ratlings.'

Ash glared at him, but Gabble didn't care. Maybe everything could still be saved. Maybe Grist could stop Ash from raiding. But the Bigrat shook his head.

'You are marked, and so you may raid.' Grist turned to the entrance, drawing down the scents. 'The sun sets. The wide world awaits.' He walked to the threshold, followed by the ratlings. Ash trotted happily after them, and Gabble, not knowing what else to do, followed. He stopped next to Ash, his paws trembling with anger, or fear, or both.

Grist turned, raising his voice to fill the chamber. 'Tonight the clanlands are yours. Hunt bravely, venture far, but do not stray beyond them. You know well that the Damplands are forbidden.' He turned a stern look to the ratlings. 'Find your prize, earn your name. Live as true rats of the clan. Or die with honour, and the Taker will guide you through the Land of Bones.' The ratlings were motionless now, every eye on Grist. 'But return dishonoured and you will live as drudges, beneath the clan's notice.' Gabble shuddered. Grist's face was grave. 'Better never to return.' In the silence that followed Grist bowed to the raiders. 'So raid well, ratlings, and may the Hunter protect you.'

Gabble hung his head. He had hoped for a reprieve, but none had come. Ratling after ratling stepped up to the entrance, whiskers twitching. To each Grist whispered, 'May the Hunter guide you,' and they ran down the slope, picking their paths and disappearing into the dusk. When it came to his turn Ash paused, one paw over the threshold, and blinked his red eyes.

'The Hunter?' he said. 'No, not the Hunter. I'll run with the Taker. Keep old Boney where you can see him, I say.' He grinned up at Grist's shocked expression, then gestured at Gabble. 'Can my brother come too?'

Grist's eyes narrowed, but he scented Gabble's coat and nodded reluctantly. 'He's barely marked. But if he wishes it, he may.' Gabble swallowed. It must have been scent from Hector, left during the fight.

Ash's eyes shone. 'Oh, that's great! We can go together, Gabbley. It'll be fun!' He turned a face full of hope to Gabble. 'You will come, won't you?'

Gabble could barely move. He stared at Ash.

'Oh, don't be such a scaredy rat,' Ash scoffed. He clapped Gabble on the shoulder. 'Come on, let's do it.'

And he raced out of the burrow, hooting with delight. Ash dashed away into the grasses, hurtling down the slope until his footfalls were swallowed by the dusk. Gabble drew an unhappy breath and made to step forward. But the big male put out a paw, halting him. Gabble saw the worry on Grist's face, smelled his concern.

'Listen, to me,' said Grist, his expression grave, 'you should return to your nest. There will be no dishonour, I give you my word.' He nodded down the path Ash had chosen. 'No rat should follow a fool. Understand?'

Gabble stared straight ahead out of the burrow, eyes narrowed against the dying sun. *I'll look after him, I promise.* That was what he had told the Mothers. He shook his head.

'He's my brother,' he said.

And he stepped into the world beyond.

chapter two

The twilight was waiting. A Hunter's sun, low and red, cast Gabble's shadow long on the ground. He ran the few paces from the tunnel to the grasses and paused there, whiskers twitching. Behind lay the colony, set beneath its high hedge, and before him the bank dropped down and away to the fields.

'Ash?' The sound fell dead into the landscape.

No response. Gabble raised his nose to the air, and took in the scents. An eternity of leaves, grass, soil, rain, food, and predators jumbled in the breeze. It was a dizzying muddle, and he shook it away. He scampered forwards, and when his foot met the hard, smooth earth of the run, familiar clan smells clustered around him once more. The runs, thank the Hunter: a network of paths imprinted on the confusion. Every patch of soil, blade of grass, or leaf that a rat touched bore scent that brought the world to order. Gabble drew down another lungful. *Here, this way, grain, water, cat, fruit, fox, avoid, meat, follow*. And a trace of Ash, faint but flowing on the breeze. Gabble scented until he was certain, and his jaw set. Ash had run off headlong into the unknown, either trusting Gabble to follow or not caring if he did. Ash had got him into this. Ash hadn't waited. But Gabble had promised: his brother, his responsibility. And with a heart-thump he was away and sprinting down the slope.

The world rushed to meet him in a spray of grass-heads. They lashed and scattered at his passing. Night noises, rustles, and cries rang in his ears. He paused, scented, listened, then put his head down and ran faster. The path split, turning to the field or continuing along the base of the slope, parallel with the hedge. Other rats had gone to the field with its short, thick stalks, bare earth, and scattered seeds: easy pickings for a rat's feast, and a good raid. But, oh, not Ash. Ash had taken the hard paths, far from the burrow and thick with danger. Gabble cursed his brother even as he followed. The run split again and again, spurs heading off to the field or up to the hedge. And each split left his own run narrower, less defined. But Ash's scent grew stronger.

Gabble settled into the rhythm of the chase. Here pause, there dash. Follow the nose, leave the eyes and ears alert for danger. Somewhere a night bird called, raucous in the distance. No danger, run faster. Gabble's muscles bunched and flowed, air burned in his lungs, and exhilaration surged in him. He was on a name raid. He was no pup, flapfoot, or ratling. He was a rat, running as a rat runs, hunting as a rat hunts. And it felt wonderful. He could run forever, or shout his joy to the gathering night. But then, abruptly, the grasses ended.

Gabble's forefeet threw up a scatter of earth. He blinked, panting, at the two scars his paws had dug into soil. Then he raised his head. Beyond a narrow verge of grass lay a wide stretch of stone, open to the sky. A chill crept in Gabble's fur. The stone surface was deathly flat and open, stretching away beneath a sparse dusting of dirt and straw. Beyond it, faded and blurred by distance, massive, square shapes reached for the sky, all steep stone sides and smooth, unbroken lines. Gabble edged deeper under cover. He had heard of this place. All of the ratlings had. Notratlan: the furthest edge of the clanlands. And beyond Notratlan all paths led to the Damplands. No ratling had ever, or should ever, come this far. Ash had, though. His scent was strong. Gabble lowered his nose to the ground, seeking the course that Ash had taken. Ash's smell billowed in the breeze, and below it Gabble detected other scents. Mouse, small vole, and something else.

Something dangerous. He froze. A moment to name it. Cat. *Oh no.* But not fresh. Faded. Enough, though, to stop the breath in his chest.

Moving as quietly as he could, Gabble rose up on his hind feet. Paws raised, ears up, he brought his head just above the grasses. He stood, quivering, listening to the dusk, every sense alert, ready to run for his life.

'Whatzit, flapfoot.' A rasping voice, right in his ear.

Gabble yelped, paddling at the air with his forepaws. He wheeled around, still flailing . . . to be greeted by the sight of Ash, white fur glimmering in the half-light, rocking with laughter. Gabble sank to all four paws, heart hammering. A mixture of anger and relief poured into him. He glowered.

'Not funny, I think.'

'It really is . . . you . . . you should have seen you jump . . .' Ash was laughing so hard he struggled to speak. He mimicked Gabble flailing about, boggling his eyes and gnashing his teeth in mock terror. 'Oh, that was *so* worth it.' Ash gestured at a knot of grasses, a few lengths from the run. 'I was hiding there for ages. I thought you'd never get here. But that was beautiful.'

Ash looked so pleased with himself that Gabble almost forgot to be angry. Almost.

'Heh,' said Gabble. He moved to the edge of the run and scanned around. No dangers that he could detect. After some moments Ash plonked himself down beside him, and together they gazed across Notratlan.

Ash cocked an eye at his brother. 'Looks good, eh?'

'No,' said Gabble. 'Not really.'

'Why? What's wrong with it?'

Ash had a perfectly innocent look on his face. The sight of it made Gabble's paws clench.

'Why did you do this?' Gabble demanded. 'We're not ready to raid. You should have waited.'

Ash scowled at him, and turned back to face Notratlan. 'It's not that easy.'

'Why not? Heh?'

'Because I'm the white rat. The one that makes the trouble.' Ash raised a paw, covered in his bright white fur, and held it, quivering under Gabble's nose. 'See? I'm different. I look different, and I smell different. And that's all I've ever been.' He placed the paw back on the ground, his expression hard, unreadable. 'But not tonight. After tonight I'll be a true rat of the clan.'

Gabble settled uneasily, unsure of what to say. It wasn't the way Ash looked or smelled that made him different. It was the things he said and the way he acted. Gabble wanted to tell Ash that, but even as he thought it he wasn't sure it was true. Instead he said, 'Heh,' and nodded at Notratlan. 'So why this? Why here?'

Ash perked up. 'Ah,' he said. 'Now I'm glad you asked me that.' He put one forepaw on Gabble's shoulder and gestured with the other at one of the giant, sky-blotting shapes at the far side of the stone expanse. 'That, Gabble, my brother. *That's* why we're here. That's what will make our raid.'

Gabble frowned. It wasn't clear what *that* was, but it looked horrible. He shook his head. 'We find food from the clanlands, we take it back for the Mothers. That's the raid.'

Ash's grin returned. 'Oh, I know. And there's food over there, Gabble. Great food. The best.'

'Who says?'

'Now, I can't tell you.' Ash winked. 'But I have my sources and, trust me, it's good.'

'And why not the field?'

'Grain and snails.' Ash dismissed the idea with a flick of his paw. 'Any drudge can feed on those. If you want respect, you do something worthy of it.'

'Ash—' Gabble began, but Ash shushed him.

'Listen. That's our future. Food from Notratlan.' And now Ash's voice held a strange note, earnest and burning cold. 'It'll *make* us, Gabble. We'll earn our names and more. We won't only be true rats, we'll be Bigrats.' Ash's eyes gleamed. 'And all we have to do is take it.'

In Ash's mouth the words were almost convincing. But misgivings churned in Gabble. A promise was one thing, but every sense told him to follow Ash no further. Gabble turned, ready to head back to the burrow. But Ash seized him with both forepaws, and pulled him close.

'Gabble, I need you. I know I've caused us trouble.' Ash's voice was low and almost pleading. 'I do, and I'm sorry. But now I can make it right, don't you see?'

Gabble stared at him. He shook his head slowly, and lifted a forepaw, pulling gently away. Ash clutched him tighter. *What a rat touches he owns.* The thought came unbidden. It was something the Mothers said. Gabble felt the strength of his brother's grip, the bond that pulled them together.

'Please, Gabble.' Ash's gaze was luminous. 'We'll have our names. We'll share them with each other and be brothers forever.' Gabble began to shake his head, but Ash gripped him harder. 'I won't let you down, I promise.' Gabble hesitated. Ash said, 'Please. Just this one thing. And if there's nothing over there, we go back with fruit or something. OK? Please?'

Gabble was never sure, afterwards, why he did it. Or what their lives would have been if he had not. But he nodded slowly.

'All right,' he said.

Ash squeezed Gabble's shoulders approvingly. 'Good rat. I'm proud of you.' Then Gabble felt Ash's paws gently pulling him around, manoeuvring him until both of them faced Notratlan, towards the tall shapes that now were all but lost in the night.

'We do this now,' said Ash, still holding him, 'and everything else is easy.' Ash's paw guided Gabble forwards. Gabble allowed himself to be walked to the edge of the cover.

'We do *what* now?'

'Like I said. We keep the Taker where we can see him.'

Ash positioned himself beside Gabble, alert and ready. Gabble looked up at the sky. The sun had gone, leaving only a faint blotch of red. The far side of the sky glowed with the first hints of moonrise. It promised to be a full moon on a clear night. A brightmoon, the Taker's moon, good for predators. They had little time before it rose to lighten the world around them.

Ash caught Gabble's expression. 'That's right. Time to run, my brother.'

And, as if the words released them, Gabble and Ash dashed together across the short grass and out onto the chill surface of Notratlan.

Chapter three

Cold stone zigzagged beneath Gabble's paws. Seed husks, fine dust, and dried grasses kicked up and settled as he passed. No clan-scent here: they were beyond the clanlands. Nothing to follow now but Ash. The sky arched away above their heads and the exposure was chilling. The feeling thrilled to Gabble's feet, making them go faster. Ahead of them towering, vertical shapes loomed against the sky, blocking the early stars. Paws on stone, breath rushing, Ash sprinting, pulling him into the heart of Notratlan. Moments later they slammed together against the massive bulk of a wall. Gabble went instantly motionless, crouched in the crook between the flat ground and the rough rock. Whiskers, ears, nose, eyes, everything was alert. Forepaws on the wall, he cautiously stood to gaze back to the clanlands. And, as if it had been waiting just long enough, moonlight splashed across the Notratlan stone, exposing every rut and hollow. Everywhere they had run now shone in the Taker's moon, right up to the ragged, black edge of the grasses.

The breeze was cold but Gabble did not move. Some sense told him not to. He caught a movement, deep in the shadows at the far side. He shrank against the wall, hoping that Ash had seen it too, that he would stay still. A black shape slunk into view. Gabble knew it immediately, without question. It was a cat, padding on soft paws towards the spot where he and Ash had begun their run. It nosed around the grasses, and the night carried the crunch and rustle of its investigations to Gabble. It crouched low, tail whisking. It batted a paw into the grass and jumped forwards. Then it sat upright with a disappointed air. It stared across to where Gabble cowered. Its eyes flashed green. Gabble held his breath. *Had it seen them? Could it smell them?*

Somewhere a fox cried. The cat's head whipped around. Another cry, shrill in the night. Then the cat sprang to its feet and ran, paws blurring, back the way it had come. It was gone. Gabble sagged against the stone wall. He reached for Ash.

'Ash,' said Gabble, 'did you see that? I—'

But Gabble's outstretched paw met nothing. He

turned to find the shadows behind him empty. While Gabble had been transfixed by the cat, Ash had simply left to explore. Gabble made a sound deep in his throat and set off. He twisted along the wall, past fallen stones and odd, metal objects, smothered by rank plants. He felt a sense of space as the wall turned a corner, followed it and was immediately greeted by the sight of Ash, visible to all, standing on top of a large, black object. Ash pawed curiously at the stones around him but then jumped off and scampered forward at Gabble's approach.

'There you are,' he said. 'What kept you?'

Gabble fought the urge to batter his brother to within an inch of his life.

'The cat, Ash.' He kept his voice as calm as he could. 'The *cat* kept me.'

Ash blinked. 'Ooh.' He stood up, looking excited. 'Cat, you say? Where?'

'At the edge of the clanlands.'

'Is it still there?'

'No. It heard a fox and ran off. But it found the grasses where we were hiding.'

Ash shrugged, losing interest. 'Good thing we were here then.'

Gabble gaped. 'But—'

'But nothing. It's like I told you, Gabbley: stick with me and it'll be fine.' And Ash bounded over to the black object he had been standing on. He jumped onto it and gestured proudly. 'I discovered this.'

The object Ash had 'discovered' was a small chamber with a hole going right through it. The black, flat side of it was slick-gritty against Gabble's paw, and gave slightly beneath his weight. The inside smelled temptingly of food. Ash's scent went through and out the other side. And something else. Gabble tensed, and glanced nervously around. He smelled rats, and not clan rats. If they discovered Ash and Gabble near their food there would be a fight. Gabble lowered his nose and scented carefully. The strange rats' scent was days old. A relief. Except that they had been all around the box, but not in. Odd. They had not fed here.

'Good, eh?' said Ash.

Gabble's head came up sharply. Ash's breath carried something, sweet like grain.

'Ash, what have you eaten?'

The words came out harder than he had intended. The grin slipped from Ash's face. 'Nothing. Just food.'

'Where from?'

Ash looked defensive. 'In there, if you must know.'

Gabble was aghast. 'Ash,' he said, 'there were no ratmarks on that food.'

Food lay all around the clanlands, and not all of it was good. Rats had died thinking they were clever, that the lack of marks meant they had found food the others had missed. What they had found was food no others would touch.

'Oh, Gabble, stop worrying, will you? It's not like I ate much. Just enough to taste.'

Gabble scrutinized Ash carefully. He seemed fine, whatever 'fine' meant in Ash's case.

Gabble shook his head. 'You are not a bright rat.'

'Then why follow me?' Ash snapped. For an instant anger twisted his features. But a moment later it was gone and Ash was cheerful again. 'Ack, it doesn't matter,' he said. 'We're not here for that food, anyway. I've got something *much* better. Come on!'

And he bounded off along the wall, following a muddy little run that was covered with scent from the foreign rats. Gabble followed him, whiskers twitching, ready to flee. Ash led him to a place where the stone wall gave way to a tall sheet of wooden slats, stretching up to be lost against the sky. The wood hung down close to the floor, but here and there were gaps, large enough for a rat to squeeze beneath. The strange rats' tracks criss-crossed the entrance, leading into the holes and back out again. Gabble sniffed curiously at the interior. Warm dusty scents, something . . .

Ash's paw rapped repeatedly down on Gabble's head. 'Whatzit, whatzit. Do I have your attention?'

'Ouch. Yes. All right.' Gabble yanked his head away

31

from Ash's paw and gave him a look. 'That hurt,' he said.

'Good.' Ash held up a paw. 'Now, I don't know if it's possible to pull off a rat's nose using only a paw, but if you don't stop sniffing at everything I'm going to have to find out. Your choice.'

Gabble sighed. 'OK, Ash.'

'Right, then.' Ash nodded at the hole. 'We, my brother, are standing at the very cusp of the greatest feat that any flapfoot or ratling has ever managed. And it's time to grasp our fate.'

And before Gabble could speak Ash scuttled off, squeezed under the wooden sheet, and disappeared into the darkness within. Gabble stared after him, wanting to chew the wood in frustration. Ash was determined to get them both killed. In a clan filled with stupid, giggling, feckless, half-witted flapfeet, Gabble just had to end up with the biggest idiot of the lot. Then he took a breath. *Look after Ash*, the Mothers had said.

'I'm trying,' he muttered. 'I'm really trying.'

And he too slipped under the wood and into the dark.

The inside was warm and hen-scented. Gabble's senses filled with straw, dust, feathers, and the few, strange ratmarks around the entrance hole. And from above, soft rustlings, and sleepy *brouk* noises. He pattered up behind where Ash stood, just beyond the threshold.

'What can you see?' Ash whispered. 'My eyes haven't adjusted.'

The place was massive. The floor was the same stone as the rest of Notratlan: flat, grey, seamless, but now coated with straw and hen droppings. Along each side raised platforms of wood stood on rows of posts. And from the heights of those platforms came the rustling of feathers and the savoury smell of chickens.

'It's hens,' whispered Gabble. 'We're in a henburrow.'

Ash turned a bright eye to Gabble. 'Indeed we are, Gabble. Just as I thought. And a henburrow means eggs.'

Gabble caught the look in Ash's eye. 'No, a henburrow means big, dangerous birdies that we leave alone.' He lowered his nose to the scant ratmarks around the threshold. The scents were fresher here. Whoever the other rats were they came in and out regularly and . . .

Ash thumped him. 'Remember the nose.' Gabble stopped scenting. 'Now,' said Ash, with an unsettling smile. 'Do you know what I'm asking myself?'

'Heh. Why you have to be a pain?'

'Very funny. No, what I'm asking myself is what two young rats could *possibly* get up to in a henburrow.'

Sometimes it was difficult to know what Ash was thinking. This was not one of those times. 'We are *not* raiding an egg.'

'Why not?' Ash switched to the voice he used when he wanted to be especially persuasive. 'Think about it, Gabble. None of the clanrats has ever come back with eggs.'

'It's impossible, I think.'

'It's not impossible,' Ash declared. 'I want egg. And I'm getting egg.'

'And how will you "get egg"? They're under the hens.'

Ash grinned, his teeth yellow in the white of his face. 'Right. So I'm going to ask them to move.'

'You're *what*?'

Gabble made a grab for his brother. But Ash danced from his grasp, hopped over some fallen straw, and scampered to the base of the first of the raised perches. Gabble dashed to stop him but Ash had already gripped the rough wood of the perch and was scrambling nimbly up it. Gabble backed away, craning for a view as Ash climbed paw over paw to the top. He hauled over the lip and plonked himself down right next to a sleeping chicken. He groomed his whiskers for a moment and then set off, dashing the length of the henburrow, threading his way between the birds. Gabble cursed under his breath and ran after him, keeping pace on the ground with the flashes of white that betrayed Ash's weaving form above. This was not going to end well. Ash's whiskers and nose were some compensation for his terrible eyesight, but in the dark he was more than capable of running headlong into a chicken.

A surprised squeak and startled clucking fractured the henburrow's quiet contentment. Gabble felt a grim satisfaction at his prediction even as his legs brought him to a skidding stop, breathless at the foot of the perch. A cacophony broke out overhead. Feathers flapped, hens' claws raked on wooden boards and squawks split the air. The sounds spread as hens each side awoke, screaming and adding to the din. From amidst the shrieking Gabble could clearly hear Ash squeaking with excitement, laughing and making 'Hah' noises.

'Ash!' Gabble shouted. 'Ash, what's happening?'

No answer.

'Ash, hold on, I'm coming.'

Gabble scanned the perches, seeking a way up, anything that would help. But Ash was far overhead and Gabble was a long way from any of the posts. In front of him a mound of straw and dirt covered the floor, but too low to be useful. Hay and dust rained down and alarm calls rang out from all sides. In moments the whole henburrow was awake and shrieking in distress.

'Below!'

Gabble threw himself to the side at Ash's warning squeak. An egg smacked into the floor by Gabble's head, splattering yolk over his whiskers. He wiped it away and glowered up at his brother.

'Not there, idiot,' Gabble shouted. 'Aim for the hay. Heh.'

Ash's white face appeared for an instant over the side of the perch.

'Sorry.'

Behind Ash a hen's long neck and sharply beaked head reared into view, ready to strike.

'Ash, look out!'

Ash twisted round and yanked his head away an instant before the hen's beak speared downward. A defiant squeak rang out and the hen fluttered backwards, clucking. It tripped, and two long-toed feet flailed above the perch. And then it was up and attacking. More flapping and squeaking.

'Coming down!'

Two objects thumped into the hay beside Gabble. He spun around to see Ash pulling himself from the hay, grinning wildly, next to an egg the same size that he was.

'Oh, *yes!*' Ash gasped. 'That was amazing!'

In moments he had shaken himself free and was grappling with the egg, trying to lever it out of the straw. Above them the chickens screamed.

'What are you doing?' Gabble demanded. 'You woke every chicken in the henburrow.'

Ash managed to roll the egg out of the hay and onto the stone floor. There it spun in a circle.

'Yes, but I have egg.'

A hen fluttered into the air and settled clumsily on the floor towards the back of the henburrow. It oriented itself and fixed them with its eye. It raised its wings, as if deciding whether to attack. Another hen flapped and settled a little further back, and regarded them beadily.

'You have egg,' Gabble hissed. 'And we're going to have beaks. Let's go.'

'Not without my egg.'

Ash shoved at the egg once more. It spun on its axis and rolled to the side. He grappled it with his paws and succeeded in pushing it a few rat-lengths towards the exit.

'Don't just stand there—help me!'

More chickens fluttered down to the floor and ran forwards, wings raised. Gabble squeaked at them and they flapped back a pace. He glanced back down the henburrow towards the entrance. Their tiny rat-hole was almost invisible. The sight made his tail go hot. Not good. Ash shoved once more at the egg and the hens tensed, lowering their heads and making a noise that was almost a growl. More hens fluttered down behind them.

'Leave the egg. They won't let us out.'

'They will. Watch.'

Ash put both forepaws against the egg and got it moving. It veered off course almost immediately, but he stepped nimbly around it, and spun it until it rolled the right way. Under Ash's guidance the egg-and-rat combination tottered with agonizing slowness down the centre of the henburrow. And behind him the chickens amassed. The clucking swelled and then died to a brooding, rustling calm. The quiet was threatening, dense with spreading wings and raking claws. Gabble began to back away. Until tonight he had never seen a hen. In the stories they were stupid, cowardly birds that were outwitted by the cunning of the rats. These, though, were not story chickens. These birds would draw blood. He risked a glance back at Ash, who had navigated the egg halfway to the hole. The movement drew an expectant shift from amidst the hens. Gabble squeaked again, glaring at them. The lead chickens flinched. Gabble turned his body sideways, keeping his eyes on the hens, and scuttled, paw over paw, after Ash, his gaze never leaving the chickens.

'Faster,' Gabble hissed when he was alongside. 'Go faster.'

'Then help me, numbskull,' Ash shot back over his shoulder.

The mere thought of turning his back on the hens gave Gabble a stabbing feeling between the shoulders.

But it would get them out of the henburrow. *Oh, Mother. Right. Time to do it.* Up on his rear paws, forefeet on the egg's smooth surface, Gabble leant his weight to Ash's. With two rats on the job the egg began to jolt and bump rapidly down towards the entrance.

'Not too fast—we'll crack it!' shouted Ash.

Gabble couldn't care less. He kept his forepaws working. He had to hop and skip to keep up with the egg, but as long as it was moving he had hope. They inched their way towards the henburrow entrance. Gabble, mouth dry and breathing laboured, began to feel the stirrings of hope. They were nearly there. They might just make it.

Wwwrraaak!

Gabble released the egg and spun about.

'Oh no,' he whimpered.

Hens were squabbling at the rear of the burrow, plucking at feathers and kicking viciously with their claws, while others rushed in mindless circles. But amidst the panic, a mass of chickens had gathered. And now it surged forwards, a monstrous beast with multiple heads and cold, glittering eyes, all fixed on Gabble.

Gabble gave a low moan and dashed to where Ash now had the egg, mere rat-lengths from the burrow entrance. Ash grinned at him.

'We did it! We're there.' The smile slipped from his

face. 'What's wrong?' Gabble grabbed Ash's shoulder and wrenched him around to face the chickens. Ash's eyes widened. 'Ah,' he said. 'Oops. Um . . . right.'

He sprinted for his egg and shoved it at the entrance hole. The egg passed easily beneath the first lip of wood and then, with a tiny creaking noise, jammed solid. Ash thrust his paws at it in frustration. It did not move.

Ash turned a desperate face to Gabble. 'It's wedged,' he said. 'We're blocked in.'

'I can see that,' Gabble snapped. 'Look. There.'

Strands of straw lay beneath the egg, enough to raise it into contact with the wood above.

'Hold the hens off,' Ash ordered, then whirled and began tugging and gnawing frantically at the wood above the egg. The clucking swelled to an angry chorus, with claws on stone, shrieks and yells as the birds came for the trapped rats. Their advance slowed now: no flailing, foolish rush, but the approach of birds that knew their prey was trapped.

Gabble squeaked in fear. He ran to help Ash, grasping for the nearest stalk and yanking backwards. The straw cut into his paws, but pulled free. He grabbed another and dragged it out from under the egg. Ash gave up on the wood and bent to the straw, working it loose from where it was pinched tight. Gabble could see the muscles in his brother's back as he strained with everything he had. Gabble glanced around. The hens pressed closer. Beak tips gleamed and yellow eyes swivelled. Wattles shook. Dust rose from feathers as they ruffled in the air, and long toes with vicious spurs scored tracks on the ground.

'Ash!' Gabble squeaked.

'Nearly done.'

'You mean done for?'

The birds hesitated, just beyond striking range, waiting for their moment. With a cry of joy Ash tugged the final piece of hay free. The egg wobbled in its hole. Ash turned to Gabble, his face alive with elation and panic.

'Let's do it,' he said.

The chickens charged. An instant's terrified impression of feathers, beaks, claws, then Gabble flung himself at the jammed egg, striking at it with all of his strength. His rear feet paddled at the dirt as he strove for purchase. And with a final, desperate heave, the egg popped free. Gabble and Ash pitched face first onto the ground. Gabble's jaw smacked painfully onto the stone floor. Then he was up and running, barging after Ash, squirming through the tiny hole and out into glorious night.

Chapter four

Gabble fell to the ground, gasping at the air. Beside his head the wooden panel rang with a series of thuds as multiple hens collided with it. The night degenerated into clucking, scratching, and pecking. Dust and straw flew out as beaks and feet poked impotently at the rathole. Gabble scrambled up, twisting away from the henburrow. He caught Ash's eye. For a moment the brothers looked at one another. Ash spluttered out a giggle. Then he was on his back pummelling his paws at the night sky and rocking with laughter. Beside him the egg wobbled to a standstill. Ash sobered slightly. He climbed to his feet and cocked an ear at the cacophony within.

'Oh dear, Gabble,' he said with mock solemnity. 'We appear to have upset the henburrow.'

Gabble found a smile on his own face. 'Something we said, you think?'

Ash winked. 'Can't see what else it could be.'

'Heh. They're oversensitive.'

'Undoubtedly.'

Gabble's breathing calmed and the smile faltered on his lips. He was still angry, he realized. He wanted to shout at Ash, to tell him never to be so stupid again. But he also wanted to grab his brother into a hug. He was proud of their raid and proud of their egg. Gabble shook his head and slumped back to the ground. He let a long, deep breath go up to the sky. They had survived. Thank the Hunter. Then his brow furrowed.

'Ash,' he said, 'how did you know about the henburrow?'

'Ah,' said Ash. He leaned a paw nonchalantly against their egg. 'I had information.'

'Yes,' said Gabble. 'But who—'

He didn't even see what happened next. One moment Ash was leaning against his egg, and the next he was down, lying winded on the floor, pinned beneath the bulk of a huge male rat. Gabble rolled up but the male whipped around to face him, baring his teeth.

Gabble hesitated, and two more rats slipped out of the shadows, placing themselves between Gabble and where the big male stood. They did not attack, but stood side-on, backs arched, blocking the way. One was a slender male, not much past being a ratling, the other a female, big with a fierce expression. Gabble shifted, weighing his options. The slender male, seeing Gabble's movement, tensed, paws up and ready to box.

'Don't move!' the male yelled. 'I call the cat on you, right?'

Gabble froze. *Call the cat on you?* For an instant he thought he saw a hint of resignation in the female's expression. But then she caught him looking and glared. Behind her Ash, labouring at the air, managed to drag in a breath. He began, feebly, to paw at his attacker. The huge male gave Ash a cuff that knocked him aside. The blow was powerful, but struck Ash across the shoulders: enough to stop his struggles, but not to hurt him.

The male looked up from Ash's prone form. 'You want to be next, flapfoot?' he demanded of Gabble. 'If not, I'd be thinking about backing off.'

One of the male's ears was flat. The other was completely missing and he bore scars along that side of his face, twisting white tracks through his fur. He arched his back aggressively. Gabble quickly weighed his options. He was facing three rats, any of them big enough to kill either him or Ash. But although Ash was completely helpless, the big male had not tried to bite him. And the other two rats weren't attacking.

Maybe they didn't really intend to hurt them. Either way, fighting would be pointless. He made his choice. Moving slowly, Gabble rolled onto his back. Maybe he could show the rats he was not a threat, but keep his feet free to defend himself. If he could get a surprise kick in, he might be able to create enough trouble for Ash to get away. Maybe.

The female settled a little, still watching Gabble closely. The slender male, though, took an aggressive step forwards.

'Come back here, Shrill,' the female ordered.

'But—'

'Do it. Now.'

The male slunk back beside her, muttering under his breath. Gabble, filled with relief, thought he caught the words 'set the cat on him'. The female gave the young male a look, then stepped forwards and regarded Gabble.

'Taker or Hunter?' she said.

'What? I don't—'

'Who do you follow: Taker or Hunter?' Gabble didn't understand the question. So he kept quiet.

'This one's not talking,' said the female. 'Scent the other one, Ar'bus.'

Gabble kept his expression neutral, but part of him was watching, and thinking. Strange. Ar'bus sounded like a true name, and she was using it as though he were the head of a clan. But there was no clan here: this was Notratlan. The big male lowered his nose and sniffed along Ash's flank. Ash flinched, glowering up at him. But he did not move. The male raised his head. 'He's a Hunter, I'd say. Time was as I could tell without sniffing. But they're all the same these days.'

Ash found his voice. 'OK, we're Hunters, if that's what you say.' He was breathing hard, but raised his head defiantly. 'So what are you going to do about it? Eh?'

The male gave a derisive snort. 'So they're Hunters, says the youngling. And what am I going to do about it, if you please?' The male swivelled his head to fix his beady stare first on Ash then on Gabble, still lying on the ground. He flexed a paw. Ash shifted position, but stopped at a jerk from the male.

'Don't try me. Old I might be, but my teeth are sharp.' He pulled his lips back, revealing strong, yellow teeth. He ground them together, making sure that Ash and Gabble got a good look.

The female stepped forwards and sniffed at the air around Gabble. 'This one smells like a Hunter to me,' she called back. Then she demanded, 'Who's your Akla, then?'

Akla. The Bossrat.

'Ged'dur,' said Gabble. 'He took it from Ar'lur when our mothers were pups.'

A twisted smile spread across Ar'bus' face. 'Ah,' he said, 'Poor old Ar'lur. Couldn't have happened to a nicer rat.'

Abruptly he straightened and stepped off Ash. Released, Ash sprang to his feet posturing aggressively with his teeth bared. The male raised a paw and Ash flinched away, fur bristling. As he backed off he collided with the young male who sent him sprawling with a shove. Ash climbed to his feet, spluttering, and squeaked a challenge.

'I wouldn't threaten him, flapfoot,' Ar'bus growled. 'Not unless you think you can win the fight.' He nodded to where Gabble lay, paws raised. 'Your friend here has it right.'

Ash shot Gabble a contemptuous look. 'I'm not doing that,' he said, glowering. 'Not for a bunch of drudges like you.'

The young male moved faster than Gabble could have believed. He battered Ash to the floor. Ash came up, panting with fury, and for a horrible moment Gabble thought he might attack. But instead Ash sidled away a few steps before crouching low, tail writhing on the ground.

'I call the cat on you,' yelled the male, his voice rising.

Ash glared and the male faced him down. A tense silence filled the air between them.

'Um, did you say "call the cat"?' asked Gabble, brightly. Still on his back with his legs in the air he must have looked ridiculous. That would help.

'Yes,' said the female, giving the young male a dirty look. 'He did. And he's probably stupid enough to do it.'

'I'm sure he is,' said Gabble. Then quickly added, 'Oh, no offence. I'd just prefer it if he didn't. You see, I'm allergic to cats. Heh.'

He had no idea where the words came from. He just knew that when he needed them, the right ones would be there. It was a knack.

A moment's confusion on the female's face. 'Allergic?' she said. 'To *cats*?'

Gabble nodded earnestly. 'They make my eyes itch. I can't stop sneezing and my nose starts running. So do my feet.' He looked from the puzzled rats to Ash, whose expression had slipped from rage down to something like exasperation. It was working. He kept talking. 'So please don't call the cat. I think they're bad for me.'

The trick was to keep a straight face. That way they could never quite tell if you were serious or not. The female sat back on her haunches, blinking. Then she shook her head and a wry smile spread across her face.

'Ah,' she said. 'A clever one. See this, Ar'bus? We've found ourselves a clever one.'

'Yes, I see,' answered Ar'bus. 'Better talking than fighting, eh? Well, you're probably right.' The old male had a considering look on his face. 'But you mind the Damplanders don't find you. Their sort don't like clever.'

Ash's head came up. 'Damplanders?' he said.

Ar'bus spared Ash only a glance. 'Scum rats and vermin,' he spat.

Damplanders. Mothers' stories to frighten pups. Rats who fought and stole from one another, who killed for pleasure. The strongest ruled and the weakest died. Rats who feared nothing, who sent enemies to the Taker, and thought that gave them honour. Gabble suppressed a shudder. Every day the Greenhedge heard rumours of rats who had gone missing, who had met Damplanders on a raid.

'Um, are there Damplanders close, then?' asked Gabble.

'Too close,' the female said. She gestured beyond the henburrow and out into the darkness. 'They eat ground birds and pond eggs. They breed and fight, and when they have no one left to fight they come here.' She grinned, and the expression had a savage edge. 'But we know how to protect ourselves. We send them to their precious Taker sooner than they'd like.'

'Yeah,' said the younger male. 'I call the cat on 'em. I do that, right, Snip?'

The female sighed. 'Yes, you do.'

Shrill brightened. 'Like now?'

'No, Shrill. I keep telling you, it's only for emergencies.' She gave Gabble, still on his back, an amused look. 'And I'm pretty sure this isn't one.'

'Thank you,' said Gabble, without quite knowing what he was saying thank you for. The female burst out laughing.

'*Thank you*, he says! What a well brought-up young rat.' She walked closer and peered down at Gabble's face. 'I think you can stand up now.'

Gabble climbed cautiously to his feet. He glanced over at Ash. A wrong word could spark trouble. And Ash specialized in that. But his brother was not paying attention, gazing instead out across Notratlan, to where the female had said the Damplanders lived.

Ar'bus too spotted the direction of Ash's gaze. He shook his head. 'Those are bad places, youngling. Damplanders kill without thought or regret. You take my advice and stay clear.' Ar'bus rose up onto his hind legs. Upright he looked huge. He gestured at the clanlands. 'Now. You have outstayed your welcome. Go back to your clan and tell them not to come here. This is Ar'bus's place, right? Ar'bus's eggs. Ar'bus's hens. Greenhedge on one side, Damplanders the other, and Ar'bus in the middle. Ready and waiting.'

'Yeah,' added Shrill. 'With his cat.'

'Shrill,' Ar'bus growled, 'if you mention the cat one more time I'll feed you to it myself.'

Shrill subsided, muttering. Ar'bus shook his head. 'The rat's obsessed,' he said. 'Right. Best you be leaving, eh? Before Shrill's obsession gets the better of him.'

Hunter, Taker, Damplanders, Ar'bus, and Snip. And Shrill and his cat. None of it made sense to Gabble. But it was clearly time to leave. He would be happy when Notratlan and its odd collection of rats was far behind him.

'Yes,' said Gabble. 'We'll go back and tell them not to come here. We're sorry we caused trouble. Aren't we, Ash?'

At the sound of his name Ash yanked his attention away from the Damplands. 'Whatever. Sorry,' he said, not sounding like he meant it. 'What about our egg?'

'It's not our egg,' said Gabble. 'It's theirs. We were wrong to take it. We'll find other food.'

'But—'

'No, Ash.' The words came out sharply. 'Not this time.'

Maybe it was the tone, or maybe even Ash could see that fighting three grown rats would be a bad idea, but for once, thankfully, he kept quiet. Ar'bus fell to all fours. He considered Gabble closely, grizzled head on one side. Then he gave a curt nod.

'You go, you pass my message,' he said, 'and I say you've earned your egg. Right?'

Gabble nodded. 'Yes,' he said. 'Thank you.'

Ar'bus gave him a twisted smile. 'Take it, then. A fee for a clever youngling.'

And then Ar'bus growled an order to Snip and Shrill. Together they scurried off to the looming wall, slipped beneath the henburrow entrance, and were gone. Gabble watched them leave. Then he walked over to where Ash was standing, looking angry and indignant.

'Drudges,' Ash spat, his lip curling. 'We should have fought them.'

Gabble thought about arguing. But there was probably no point.

'Never mind, Ash,' he said. 'At least we've got egg.'

The Taker's moon had set and dawn was lightening the sky by the time Gabble and Ash had rathandled their egg to the foot of the Greenhedge slope. A dull drizzle fell, making everything damp. They had shoved, lifted, rolled, cajoled, dragged, and slid their cumbersome prize all the way from Notratlan, and Gabble was utterly sick of it. He was sick of being wet, sick of hiding at the slightest noise, sick of the feeling that any moment something large and hungry could attack them. And above everything he was completely fed up of rolling this Mother-forsaken egg. He ached everywhere, all of his paws were sore, and the one he had cut on the straw throbbed, hotly. Burrs and bits of stick had caught in his fur and his legs were plastered in mud. But he knew one thing: he was going to get this egg back home if it killed him. And they had almost made it. Just this one final slope and it was done.

Gabble let go of the egg and staggered a few paces to the side to get a better look up the run. It disappeared up through the grasses to where the hedge stood, silhouetted against a lightening sky. The way looked like it should be smooth enough and not too slippery. A feeling of satisfaction spread through him. The Mothers would be proud of them. Ash, against all expectation, had been right. They truly had done something exceptional.

Gabble glanced at his brother and frowned. Ash was a worry. More than usual. He was still pawing vaguely at the egg, trying to roll it on his own. His forelegs worked, but his eyes were glazed and his face slack.

'Ash,' said Gabble, gently, 'we've stopped. Heh.'

Ash put his head on one side, as if he had heard something he had not understood. Then he lifted his paws from the egg. 'Why?' he asked.

'Because we're nearly home,' said Gabble. Ash swayed slightly, shaking his head as if to clear it. Gabble watched him, concerned. 'Are you all right?'

Ash stared, but didn't respond. Gabble couldn't remember when, exactly, Ash had stopped talking but his brother had been getting quieter all night. He had started by subjecting Gabble to a tirade of abuse for having rolled over for those other rats. Where, he had demanded, was Gabble's spine? According to Ash, they could have fought off the others, but only if Gabble had stood up for himself. Honestly, he had said, sometimes he wondered if Gabble would ever understand. That Gabble agreed with. He didn't think he'd ever understand either. But while Ash was being irresponsible and obnoxious he was at least being, well, Ash. The night had left behind a rat who was unrecognizably different. He answered only when spoken to, and when he did his words were dreamy and vague. He moved as though sleepwalking: paws moving automatically, eyes staring inward. And on Ash's breath Gabble could detect that same sweet smell of the food he had eaten outside the henburrow. The thought would not leave him: what if that food had been bad for rats?

Ash blinked. He focused on his brother. 'Gabble,' he said. His head swung in an arc as he registered their surroundings. 'Hedge. And we have egg. That's right, isn't it?'

'Yes, Ash. We have egg.'

'Good.' He swung his head around again, taking

in the hedge and the run leading up. He nodded to himself, shaking off some of the lethargy. 'Then let's get it to the burrow.'

That was more like it. Gabble's muscles complained at the thought, but he ignored them and positioned himself behind the egg.

'OK,' said Gabble. 'Home.'

It took lots of shoving, panting and manoeuvring to get the thing moving up the hill. And Gabble found himself taking the bulk of weight. Ash was exhausted and needed constant breaks. But eventually, legs shaking and chests heaving, they toppled the egg over the lip and into the burrow entrance. They turned it end on to fit into the tunnel, and eased it down the passage and into the raid chamber. Ash staggered over to the wall and hunched there, breathing heavily. Gabble, though, was too happy to notice. They had done it! They had made the best first raid that any rat had ever managed. And they had done it younger than any other rats ever. It was over. The only thing left was to take their prize to the Mothers.

Gabble could almost dance for pride. He ran to Ash's side, to rouse him into helping with the egg. But Ash did not move, not even a flick of an ear. He was so still that for a horrible moment Gabble thought he was dead. But then above the grunts and squabbles of the burrow he heard the sound of Ash's breathing.

His brother's ribs rose and fell, accompanied by a faint crackling noise from deep in his chest. *Oh, not good.* Gabble nudged him again.

'Ash?'

No response.

'Ash?'

Nothing. Gabble put a paw on him and Ash rocked back, shakily, with its weight. He half opened one eye.

'Ash? Say something.'

Ash closed his eye. He slumped further against the wall, and drew in a breath that crackled. Gabble stared at him in horror. And then he ran, staggering on his exhausted muscles, dashing for the tunnel that led down to the Mothers' chambers.

Chapter five

Gabble pulled his thin covering of fur and grass tighter around him until it was almost warm enough to sleep. For two days he had nested here, in this nook in the burrow wall. For two days Ash had lain in the nest chamber, feverish and ill, eyes tight shut, sleeping as if dead. And for two days the breath had rattled in Ash's body as though bones had come loose inside him. The Mothers had watched over him the whole time, keeping him warm.

Gabble had given up trying to get into the nest to see his brother. Every time he did, the Mothers blocked his way. 'No, Gabble,' Bustle had said. 'A Mother's chamber is no place for a rat who has raided. You are no longer a pup to sleep in our nest.' And Whisker's look, sorrowful but determined, had told him all he needed to know. *You tried, Gabble. You had your part to play, and now we must have ours.* The pair of them stood together and he could not argue. They didn't blame him, they said. Nobody could expect to have a say in what Ash said or did. But somewhere, deep in a place that none of them would speak of, they all knew that Gabble had failed. He had broken his promise. And so he had lowered his gaze and left, dragging his tail behind him.

Two Mothers. Some rats had two, some more, and some only one. Females who had made the promise to be Mothers together, to share fates and raise their litters. They were his Mothers and Ash was his brother, the only survivors of their litter. And now Gabble was alone. He was no longer a flapfoot, protected by their scent, but also not a true rat of the clan. He had been marked and had raided, but had not yet been granted his name. The spaces in the clan's fabric had closed him out, leaving him to squeeze uncomfortably around their edges.

Gabble turned over, trying to find some warmth. The eggshell lay in the tunnel beside him, empty and discarded. The Mothers had eaten his offering, as was proper for a name raid, and then left him. He pressed himself further back into the hollow and closed his eyes. He knew he should be hungry, but right now all he wanted was sleep and some peace away from the noise of the colony. Not that he could escape from that. Even down here, where the squeaks and chatter were muted almost to silence, it rang loud in his ears, a reminder that he didn't belong any more. Sleep dragged at him and the clan sounds warped around his thoughts. The world began to drift away.

'Hey, you.'

Words. Maybe for him. He tried to open his eyes, to shake free of the sleep. Something struck his shoulder, hard.

'I said, "Hey, you." Are you deaf?'

Words again. Gabble tried to rouse himself, but it was hard.

'Don't ignore me. It's rude.'

Gabble opened his eyes, struggling to focus. Whiskers, eyes. Lots of disordered hair. The face of a female, scowling down at him.

'Rude,' Gabble repeated, vaguely. 'Is it?'

'Of course,' said the female, giving him a stern look. 'Are you stupid?'

'Probably,' he said. Gabble staggered to his feet, trying to focus. The female was big with long limbs, big paws, and fur that stood up in all directions. For a moment he wondered if she was an adult, but then he caught her smell. She was a young ratling, probably not much older than he was, but massive. And annoyed about something. She put her head on one side.

'Awake, are you?' she asked.

'I am now. Heh.'

'Good,' she said, briskly. 'I'm looking for Gabble.'

'Why?'

'None of your business,' she said. 'Just tell me where he is. Then you can go back to whatever it is you do here.'

Anger brought Gabble fully awake. Whoever this female was he was sure he didn't deserve her. Not on top of everything else. He regarded her for a moment, then put on a frightened expression.

'Gabble, you say?'

The female raised her eyes to the ceiling. 'Yes. Gabble.'

Gabble glanced around nervously. 'Hush, lower your voice. Gabble's not the sort of rat you want to be shouting about. Not around here.'

'What are you talking about?'

'Hush, I said,' Gabble whispered. 'I don't think that I should tell you where he is. He'll be angry with me.'

'Don't be ridiculous. He's just a flapfoot, like you.'

The words 'like you' stung, but he kept his expression nervous. He could hear the uncertainty in her voice.

'Gabble's no normal flapfoot,' he said, giving a mock shudder. 'He's a brute. Vicious. I wouldn't go looking for him if I were you.'

The female stared. For a moment Gabble thought

she was going to swallow the whole story. Then her eyes narrowed. 'You,' she said, 'are an idiot. I'm going to find someone else to ask.' And she stalked off.

'Good idea,' said Gabble to her retreating form. He settled back down in his hollow and closed his eyes. If he was any less tired he should probably be wondering why a strange female ratling was looking for him. But he wanted rest. He let his breathing calm and slipped back into sleep.

He was woken by a firm smack across the head.

'Ouch!'

'Ouch yourself,' said the female. She did not look pleased.

'What does that mean?' Gabble demanded. He pulled himself to his feet and rubbed at his ear where she had caught it. 'And you shouldn't hit people, I think.'

'Why didn't you tell me who you were?'

Ah, so she had found someone else to ask, then.

'Because you were nasty to me. Heh,' he said. 'Now, what do you want?'

'*I* don't want anything,' she said.

'If you don't want anything why are you bothering me?'

'Because my father wants to talk to you.'

Gabble could feel his temper fraying. 'And who's your father meant to be?' he demanded.

'Ged'dur. The Akla.'

Gabble froze. The Bossrat. And of *course* he wanted to talk to Gabble. He stared at the ratling until he was sure it wasn't a joke. And then a cold panic gripped him. What had he done? The Bossrat never concerned himself with the flapfeet. But despite everything a small hope blossomed in him. Perhaps the Akla knew of his raid and might grant him his name. Or, alternatively, maybe he was angry and about to throw Gabble out of the Greenhedge. The female saw Gabble's expression and smirked. Gabble cast a wistful look at the entrance to the nest. He wanted nothing in the world so much as to crawl back, curl up, and stay there until it all went away. And preferably to say something to this female first that would wipe the smug look off her fluffy face.

But he said, 'You'd better take me to him, then, hadn't you?'

'Tell me, Gabble. Do you know what makes me Akla?'

Gabble, standing nervously inside the entrance to the Akla's chamber, stared at the Bossrat's massive frame. He swallowed. The Akla's scent spoke of authority, and he gave an impression of brute physicality and quick intelligence. And Gabble couldn't help noticing that the hair on his rump was covered with scars.

'They call you "Gabble" for a reason, I take it?' said the Akla, mildly.

Gabble nodded. 'Yes,' he managed. 'Sorry.'

The Akla waved the apology aside. 'So what do you think it is?'

'The reason I'm called Gabble?'

'No. What makes me the Akla.'

'You're bigger than everyone else.' The words spilled out before he could stop them.

The Akla frowned. For a moment Gabble wondered if he had gone too far. But then the Akla nodded, curtly.

'That helps, I won't deny it. But you need more than one type of strength.'

The huge rat ushered Gabble further into his chamber. As Gabble stepped forward the Akla pattered around behind him and back towards the entrance. There he cocked an ear, listening in silence for some moment.

'Can you hear that?'

The chamber lay in the very heart of the Greenhedge. From every direction noise poured in: paws on soil, squabbling, laughing, chatter, cries, squeaks, snoring, muttering, digging. All of the hustle of the clan met here. Gabble nodded.

'Yes, sir.'

'And what do you hear?'

'The clan.'

The Akla nodded. 'Yes. But you'd be surprised how many do not. I ask them this question and they cannot answer. They barely feel the soil beneath their feet. They follow the scents without thought. But that does not mean there is no soil or scent.' The Akla's eyes glinted as he spoke, fixed on Gabble's face. 'Our clan has many rats, living blindly, thinking of themselves. But the clan is more than any one rat. It is the cradle in which our lives are held. It binds us.' The Akla held Gabble's gaze. 'What makes me Akla is that I see that.'

The Akla settled in the threshold. 'I hold the names of the true rats of the Greenhedge. And in so doing I carry the clan's concerns. That is my function. And right now, Gabble, *you* are my concern.'

That didn't sound good. Gabble cast a glance over the Akla's shoulder, but the exit was firmly blocked.

'I hear of unsettling events,' the Bossrat continued. 'My Bigrat, Ro'nar—Grist—tells me of two flapfeet who were marked with the ratlings' respect and who undertook a name raid.'

Gabble dared not blink. The Akla continued. 'But flapfeet on a name raid is unheard of, so I dismissed the tale. Wise of me, don't you think?'

Gabble nodded, uncertainly.

'And then came the morning. And I hear that Ro'nar's tale was indeed true, and that two flapfeet raiding that night returned with an egg. A feat that surely must be to their credit.'

Abruptly the Akla rose and paced forwards until

he was uncomfortably close to Gabble. His whiskers twitched as he inhaled the scents from Gabble's coat. His gaze never wavered from Gabble's eyes. When he was finished he gave a small grunt and pushed past Gabble back into his chamber.

'Something here is not as it should be, Gabble,' said the Akla. 'I asked myself why a flapfoot might name raid. I found no answer. I summoned you, and I smell the merest smudge of ratlings' respect. Enough to raid perhaps, but little enough, also, to permit a sensible flapfoot to return to his burrow.'

Gabble kept his face impassive. Some sense told him that if he opened his mouth too wide trouble would walk into it. But the Akla's impassive gaze bored into him, and the silence ached to be filled. 'I didn't want to raid, sir. I went to look after my brother.'

The Akla's features twisted into a smile, but he did not look amused. 'This I know,' he said. 'I spoke with Hector this morning, but well before then I had heard tales of the white flapfoot who wanted to raid.' The smile disappeared, leaving the Akla's face stony. 'It's no mystery why you raided, Gabble. The trouble lies with the egg. You see, there are two places, and two only, within a night's journey where a raider may find such a prize. One lies deep in the Damplands, where the water birds nest.' The Akla put his head on one side, watching him closely. 'Your egg did not come from there, not unless you have discovered some previously unknown type of water chicken. And for this we should all be grateful.'

Gabble blinked. 'Should we?'

'Yes. Very. If you had stolen so much from the Damplanders you would not now be talking to your Akla. You would be speaking with the Taker himself. And for the Greenhedge the outcome would be war, bloody and terrible. For a flapfoot to venture so far would be an insult to the Damplanders' clan.'

The Akla's eyes narrowed. His tail twitched on the floor.

'The alternative,' he continued, his voice becoming harder, 'is that you went to Notratlan, slipped into a henburrow, thieved an egg, and spent the night rolling it back here. This is what you did, and it was extremely stupid.' Gabble said nothing, but flushed hot beneath his fur. 'Notratlan is not ours to raid,' said Ged'dur, 'and nor is it the Damplanders'. It is a deadly place upon which neither clan treads. And it is good that we don't go there. The fear of it keeps our clans apart. And were that fear for one instant to dissipate . . .'

The Akla let the words hang. Gabble stared at him, the full significance of his and Ash's actions unfurling in his mind. He thought about Ar'bus and what he had said of the Damplanders. He thought about his scent and Ash's all over the henburrow, and what would happen if a Damplander went there and smelled it. He wondered if the Akla knew about the rats who already lived in Notratlan. And he remembered the message Ar'bus had given him to pass on. He almost opened his mouth to speak, but some sense told him to keep silent.

'Tell me but one thing, Gabble,' said the Akla. 'Did you or the white rat, your brother, take one step beyond Notratlan? Did your feet tread upon a Damplander's run?'

Gabble shook his head. 'No.'

'Are you certain?'

'Yes, I promise.'

The not-really-a-smile reappeared on the Bossrat's face. He leaned forwards and carefully scented Gabble's paws. His whiskers ruffled Gabble's fur and his own scent, powerful and musky, filled Gabble's nostrils. Gabble leaned aside, averting his gaze. The Akla withdrew, looking satisfied.

'That is well,' he said. 'And so I think I need not worry.' He answered Gabble's questioning look with an impatient gesture. 'Gabble, in this clan we have two idiotic flapfeet who not only attempted a name raid but went to Notratlan. If you had been ratlings, bearing the full Greenhedge scent, and if you had then stepped into the Damplands, smelling as you did of Notratlan, then my time as the Greenhedge Akla would have ended in war.' The Akla bared his teeth. 'As it is, you risked my clan for an egg. You will not do that again.'

Gabble quickly nodded, eyes downcast.

'You were lucky,' said the Bossrat. 'And so were we all. For this reason you escape further punishment. Now return to your Mothers and breathe no word of this to anyone.' He turned away. 'This is my decision. Now you may leave.'

Gabble glanced up. 'But—' he began.

The Akla's attention snapped back. 'You no-say me?'

'Our names,' Gabble squeaked. Then he straightened. *Rather die than live as a drudge.* He raised his chin and looked the Akla in the eye. 'Please. We raided. We should have our names. I ask not for myself but for my brother. He's ill. He might . . .' Gabble faltered, swallowing against sorrow that welled in his throat. 'He might need a name for the Taker.'

In two quick steps the Akla was on him. A heavy blow from the Akla's hind foot thudded into Gabble's flank. Gabble squeaked and scrabbled away. He shrank against the burrow wall, a bruised ache blossoming where the Akla's paw had struck him.

'Being an Akla is to maintain balance,' said the Akla, his voice calm and level, as though he had barely moved. 'I balanced your age against your stupidity and let your transgression pass. And still you ask more

68

of me?' Then he sighed, and for an instant Ged'dur looked weary. 'You asked for one who may die. That is well. And you raided Notratlan. It was foolish, but brave.' He gestured to Gabble's flank. 'There. You bear my mark. Take it to your Mothers, to exchange for your name.'

'Thank you,' said Gabble. He began to turn, but before he could move the Akla spoke.

'Remember this: you will carry a name that you scarcely deserve. And if you no-say me again, or by your actions threaten my clan, I will not hesitate to act. Do you understand me?'

'Yes, sir,' said Gabble.

'Good. Do not disappoint me.'

'No,' said Gabble. 'Thank you.' And he backed out of the chamber.

The Akla's daughter escorted Gabble back to his family burrow. She looked thoroughly annoyed about it. Gabble had tried to say that he knew the way and she could go back home if she wanted, but she snapped that it wasn't her choice to be there. After that they moved in silence, scrabbling their way along the labyrinth of tunnels, skirting any passages that led to the heart of home-burrows, keeping to the open routes. These were all clanrats, but that did not mean two youngsters could go wherever they wanted. You kept away from the nest chambers, and if you smelled newborns then it was simpler, and safer, to take the high paths above the ground. But Gabble barely registered where his feet led. His thoughts were heavy, as though too many were stuffed into his head. The Akla who had granted his name, his angry daughter, the way the Mothers were acting, Damplanders, war, Ar'bus and his small clan, and Ash, ill, perhaps dying: all a miserable mess from which he longed to escape.

'You have his mark.' She had been quiet for so long that it took Gabble a moment to realize the Akla's daughter had spoken. Her words sounded almost like an accusation. 'He granted you your name, didn't he?'

Gabble nodded.

'But he wanted something else.'

Gabble did not answer, but stepped around a stone.

'Any of the Bigrats can grant a name,' she persisted. 'It doesn't need to be the Akla. What did he want?'

'He had some things to ask me.' The muscles of his flank ached as he walked. He ignored them.

The female rolled her eyes. 'Well, *obviously*. But what?'

Gabble shook his head. 'I can't tell you. Sorry.'

The Akla's daughter gave Gabble a filthy look. Then she hit him: a flurry of blows, hard, across the head.

'Hey!' Gabble jerked away from the onslaught. She was big and it hurt. 'What are you doing?'

70

She fell back to all fours and shrugged. 'You didn't tell me what I wanted to know.'

'And hitting me helps, does it?'

'Yes. I feel a lot better.' She hit him again for good measure.

Gabble raised a paw, without knowing quite what he might do with it. 'Please stop,' he said.

'Why?'

'Because I don't like it. Heh.'

'And I don't like not being told things.'

Gabble glared. And then, abruptly, he realized he didn't care any more. He lowered the paw back to the floor. 'It isn't my fault,' he told her. He turned and walked away.

After a moment she fell in beside him. 'What isn't your fault?'

'This. Any of it.'

Two turns brought Gabble to a familiar corner. He pattered down a little passage that joined with the tunnel leading to the raid chamber. To his left, the tunnel grew brighter. To his right, the chamber sloped down to a series of gloomy intersections, finally leading down to three families' burrows. The furthest and smallest would bring him to the Mothers, and Ash. He swallowed, hard, against the unhappy feeling that rose up his throat. His vision blurred and he blinked until it cleared. Then Gabble gestured at the tunnel.

'My home's down there,' he said. But the words came out thickly, and even as he said them he wondered if they were still true.

'Yes, I know.' The female spoke slowly, as though talking to an idiot. 'That's where I found you.'

'And my brother,' said Gabble. 'I—I think he might die.'

The words lingered in the chamber, as if caught among the mud and stones. They sounded terribly real.

The female stared. 'Oh,' she said. 'That's bad.'

'Yes.' Gabble nodded, not taking his eyes from the tunnel. 'It is.'

'How . . . I mean, why?'

'On the raid. He ate something. It think it poisoned him. Or maybe it was the fight.' Gabble shrugged, miserably. 'With Ash it could have been anything.'

'He sounds like trouble.'

Gabble bristled. Ash was his brother to criticize, not hers.

'I want you to go now, please,' he said.

The female tensed as if ready to hit him again. But she simply said, 'I can't.'

'Why not?'

'I am the Akla's daughter. One day I shall be clan Mother. I must witness the naming.'

Oh. So she would have to be there.

'Fine,' said Gabble. 'Come on, then.'

She followed him a few paces down the tunnel.

'I have a name, you know,' she said.

'Yes. Heh. I'm sure you do.'

'It's Feather.'

There was something about the way she said it. Gabble heard defiance in her voice, daring him to comment. He carefully did not glance at her big, muscular frame and abundant, disordered fur.

'That's a nice name.'

'Are you trying to be funny?' she demanded.

'Not really.'

'I suppose that's OK, then.'

And together they dropped down the tunnels, making for the family chambers. As Gabble approached the nest, the Mothers rushed out, preventing him from going further. He stood before them feeling strange, with Feather at his back. He had never thought about it before, but gazing at their drawn, worried faces, he realized that they looked quite different from one another. They had always simply been the Mothers, with their homely scent and comforting presence, their soft words in the darkness. And now he stood on the threshold of becoming a true rat. He wondered how things would be now between them.

'I'm sorry, Mothers,' he said. The words came out scratchily. He cleared his throat. 'I seek my name. I am of the Mother. I carry her heart. I am of the Hunter and have earned his mark. I ask for my name. And I ask for my brother who cannot speak.'

Those last words were meant for those who had died raiding, so they might have honour in death. They were not right, here, but they would earn Ash his name.

The Mothers exchanged glances. Whisker nodded to her sister. 'I will do this,' she said. 'You see to Ash.' Bustle nodded and turned without a word, slipping back into the nest.

Whisker stepped forwards to greet her son, and scented his flank. Her eyes widened.

'The Akla?'

Gabble nodded. 'Yes. You're my birth mother?'

Whisker smiled. 'Yes.' Then she said, formally, 'I gave you life, and I named you. This name I now give you.' She stepped forwards and brought her mouth to his ear, speaking words that were only for him. 'My name is Na'sta. You are my Fo'dur.' Then she turned to Feather. 'He will speak his name. He is my son and a true rat of the Greenhedge.'

Gabble turned to Feather. 'My name is Fo'dur,' he said.

Feather replied, 'Fo'dur, as hereafter the Akla shall know you.' Then she pushed past Gabble, and entered the nest where Bustle was waiting. From within Gabble heard voices—Bustle's then Feather's, indiscernible through the wall—and Feather emerged once more.

She looked at him for a moment, an odd expression on her face, then turned to Whisker.

'I am sorry. I have witnessed this naming, but the other . . .'

Whisker swallowed, but nodded. 'I understand,' she said. 'Ash cannot speak his name. But if he wakes may we call you?'

Feather gave her a look full of pity. 'As soon as he does,' she said. Then she bowed. 'I have witnessed Fo'dur's name and shall carry it to the Akla.'

Whisker bowed in turn. 'Thank you,' she said. 'You will always be welcome in my burrow.' Feather smiled at her. Then she gave Gabble an unreadable look, whisked about, and ran for the tunnel, her fur trailing behind her. When she was gone Whisker laid her chin over Gabble's shoulder, and twined her paws in his fur. She pulled him close and held him, leaving her scent to seal his name.

'My Fo'dur,' she whispered.

Fo'dur. He felt the knowledge settle in him. In old rat it would have been two words: *fol edur.* It meant 'the one who shines'. A good name. He returned the hug for some moments, before gently prising himself free. He held her at paw's length, unsure of whether to smile or to cry.

'I'm proud of you, Gabble,' said Whisker.

'Thank you,' he managed. 'May I tell Ash?'

Whisker looked quickly away. 'If you will.' Her whiskers trembled a little, but her voice was steady. 'But he will not hear you. He may never hear anything again.'

A small sound escaped Gabble's lips. He swallowed, quickly. 'Then I'll tell him anyway,' he said. 'We should share the naming.'

'Gabble, you need to be sure,' said Whisker. 'You know what it means.'

Gabble nodded. To share a naming was to twine your lives, bound by birth and choice. 'He wanted it.'

'I'm sure he would have.' And now Whisker's voice held a hint of her usual dryness. 'But I never thought that what Ash wanted was the best for you.' She sighed. 'Ah, but what harm can it do, now? All right. Go to him. He would have liked it.'

Gabble nodded and turned to face the small nest. Its presence gave him a tight feeling in his chest. He and Ash had been born there. He didn't want to think that his brother might die in there too. He had failed to protect Ash, but he could still do this duty. Gabble stepped over the threshold. Ash was in the centre, hunched over on himself and motionless, amidst collected bits of fur and dried grass. His head was down, held beneath his paws and covered with bedding. The only part of him that showed was one ear, flat against his head, where Ash's birth mother crouched, whispering to her son. At Gabble's approach she straightened. She regarded Gabble for some moments.

'So you want to tell Ash your name,' said Bustle. 'I tried to give him his. Whether he heard or not I can't say.' She made to step past Gabble, then hesitated. 'Gabble, I shall always be your mother too,' she said.

Gabble nodded, unable to speak. She put a paw on him, then pattered past and out of the nest. Gabble went and stood awkwardly at Ash's side. He hesitated, his paws above the cover of stems, almost afraid to touch his brother. Then he began to clear away the grass. Ash's fur felt cold. He did not move, not even a twitch. Gabble couldn't tell even if he was breathing; not until Ash's sides swelled and a breath crackled faintly in him. Gabble lowered his lips to his brother's ear, uncertain of whether Ash could hear.

'Ash, it's me,' said Gabble. 'It's Gabble.' Gabble thought he felt a movement under his paw. Or maybe he wanted to believe that he had. 'I'm here,' Gabble said, filling the silence with words. 'I'm sorry. I wanted to look after you, but I couldn't. And now you're . . .'

Gabble raised his eyes to the roof of the chamber. Stupid. So much he could say, and the only words that would come out were useless. Where were the right words, the ones he always had when he needed them?

'Ash, I need you. I need you to be as you were. You

said we would keep the Taker where we could see him. I need you to do that for me now.'

As he spoke, Gabble's paws continued, gently disinterring his brother's body. Grass fell from Ash's shoulders, from around his back and his tail. Still Ash remained hunched, head beneath his paws. Gabble kept talking.

'Ash, the raid worked. The Bossrat heard about it. He granted us our true names. We're rats. You and me. We did it.'

Gabble placed a paw softly on his brother's shoulder.

'I'll tell you my name, if you'd like? And if you tell me yours we'll always be brothers. What do you say?'

He lowered his lips to Ash's ear.

'My name is Fo'dur,' he whispered. 'It means "shining one", or something.' Ash's breath crackled. For an instant Gabble thought he saw a paw flex. But perhaps he had imagined it. His paw twisted in Ash's white hair. He regarded it a moment. 'Strange, isn't it? In some ways I think my name would suit you better.'

Ash gave no sign that he had heard. Gabble watched him for some moments. Apart from the crackle of his breathing, the nest was silent.

Gabble straightened and raised his voice. 'I would have liked to have heard your name. But maybe later.' He took his paw from Ash's shoulder. 'Sleep well, Ash.'

Gabble turned away from his brother's still form.

He hung his head. He was a rat. He had his name. He was Fo'dur and he must not cry. Ash might still come back to them. He might.

'Fight the Taker,' said Gabble, speaking loudly to the air. 'You are not his. Not yet.'

He stepped away, making for the exit. But was stopped dead by a soft rustle of grasses. There, again. A slow noise, as of stiff muscles moving. Gabble spun back, heart leaping. Ash's paws had unfurled from over his eyes. In the dim light they seemed crusted with something, and stained darkly. Gabble rushed forwards and brushed the remaining stems from Ash's form, running his paws over his brother's fur. Ash opened like a blossom, shakily, paws coming away from his face. The face they revealed was crusted red and blotchy, with eyes closed, sealed shut.

'Ash?' Gabble hesitated, paws raised above his brother.

Ash's mouth moved. He made an unintelligible noise. Then he coughed, with a weak bubbling sound. His mouth moved again. And this time a name came out.

'Gabble.'

'Ash! You're awake.'

His mouth moved. The words were slurred, difficult to hear. 'Am I?'

'You're speaking,' said Gabble, half laughing, and

desperately grooming the last of the hay from his brother's fur. 'It's a start.'

Ash coughed again, stronger this time, with a hacking noise. His whole body went tense, and then subsided.

'I . . . I don't feel good.'

Gabble regarded Ash's crusted cheeks and red-stained paws.

'You don't look good. Heh. But you're back.'

'Back,' Ash repeated. 'My eyes.'

'They're closed. They're stuck shut, I think.'

Ash raised his forepaws and began to paw at the crust around them. Then he stiffened and made a small moaning sound. Gabble grasped Ash's paws.

'Ash, what is it?'

Ash clutched for Gabble. He twisted free from Gabble's grip and grabbed at his forelegs with feverish strength. His paws wrenched at Gabble's fur.

'I saw him!' Ash cried. 'He's coming.'

Gabble pulled back, but was held fast. 'You saw who?'

Ash shook his head blindly. 'I saw him,' he repeated.

'Ash, it's all right. There's no one there. No one's coming.'

'*He* is.' Ash was breathing heavily, his chest crackling. 'He's coming.'

'Who's coming?' Gabble said.

'The Taker. The Taker's coming.'

'Ash—'

'I saw him!' Ash shouted. 'I saw his Land of Bones.'

Gabble stared, horrified. 'Ash,' he managed, 'you're ill, it's—'

Ash yanked him closer. 'No!' he shouted. His breath rasped and crackled in his lungs. 'It was him. The Taker.'

Then Ash released his hold and Gabble staggered back. Ash collapsed, panting, into the grasses.

'It was terrible,' Ash said, quietly. 'Terrible.'

And as Ash spoke a single, red tear squeezed out from beneath his eyelid. It trickled down over the crusted streaks on his face, a brilliant crimson against his fur. Then Ash covered his face once more. The chamber filled with the bubble of his laboured breath, and the approach of the Mothers' paws, frantic in the tunnel beyond.

Chapter six

The colony emptied in ones and twos. Rats appeared at entrances and lingered before bounding away to their foraging grounds. From his vantage point below the hedgetop Gabble could just make out their greyish shapes, and the pause–run of their movement. Somewhere below him a pair of flapfeet boxed and rolled in the safety of the hedge, before being admonished by their mother. Gabble listened, wondering how they could be so young.

Ash's breath rasped in the air, and Gabble half-turned to him. Ash too was staring after the dispersing forms. In the moonglow the stains around his eyes were black, like sunken pits in his skull from which his eyes themselves glittered. Ash looked a fright. The clan's new pups avoided him, and whispered when he passed. They were frightened by his face and his rattling breath. But at least he was getting stronger. And, naturally, doing his very best to give everyone the impression he was fine. He had already tried heading down to the field and had been dragged back to the burrow, wheezing and choking. Even Ash had admitted defeat, then. But still, here he was, gazing after the other raiders and itching to join them.

'Whatzit, Gabble.' Ash caught Gabble's eye. He looked half amused, half annoyed. 'Can I help?'

Gabble shook his head. 'No. Sorry.'

'If you keep staring at me like that I'm going to get a headache.' Ash tried a grin. It looked ghastly. 'Stop worrying, will you? I'm OK, I promise.'

But then his breath bubbled in his ribs and he hunched over, coughing and hacking. When, eventually, the fit passed he straightened.

'Ouch,' said Ash.

'Heh. That's you being OK, is it?'

'It will be if I can get rid of this cough.'

'You've only had a little time. You will need more, I think.'

'That's what you said yesterday.'

'Yes. It was true then too.' Gabble nudged Ash with a paw. 'We should feed. I'm hungry.'

A night breezed ruffled their fur. Ash's whiskers twitched.

'Food, eh? What do you reckon? Notratlan and eggs?'

'Hedge and snails,' said Gabble, firmly. 'Especially if you're going to keep coughing.'

Ash pulled a face. 'Hedge and snails. My favourite.' But he walked up the incline to the meshed twigs and thorns of the hedgetop. Gabble followed, pretending not to notice how long it took, or how his brother's legs shook with the effort. Then they set to work finding something to eat, eventually locating an unfortunate slug and some grass seeds. They chewed the slug together. It tasted nasty, but Gabble didn't complain. It was food, and Ash needed to heal.

Ash brought a kernel up to his mouth. His paws shook so badly that it took him several attempts. Then he fumbled for another, and glared as it bounced down the slope beyond his reach.

'Oh, what's the point?' Ash gestured angrily at the hedge and the kernel. 'Just look at this. Hiding in hedges like an old, toothless rat. Is this all I've got?'

Gabble said nothing. Sometimes that was best.

Ash gazed off down the slope. A muscle in his shoulder twitched. 'I never feared the Taker. You know that, don't you?'

'Yes,' said Gabble. 'I know that.'

Ash had barely spoken of his illness, and cut short any attempt to talk about it. Maybe he still thought he seen the Taker and maybe not, but Gabble didn't really care. He just wanted his brother to get better. But whatever fever dream had gripped Ash had left teeth in his flesh and shadows in his mind. He was still Ash, but lessened, somehow, as if something vital had leached away. It was true that he had never feared the Taker. But he did now.

Something further along the hedge made a skittering sound, like a pebble rolling or loose soil sifting downward. Gabble stared down the length of the hedge. There, almost lost amidst the thickest cover, he spied a suspicion of a rat's whiskers. He squinted, and saw a tail, sticking out from beneath a branch. It was a rat, and doing a terrible job of staying hidden. As he watched, it slipped from cover and slunk closer, keeping to the dark but moving clumsily.

'Ash, look.'

Ash, pawing at grain, barely glanced in his direction. 'What?'

'Over there. A rat.'

'We have lots of them, Gabbley. It's called a "clan".'

'Funny. Heh. But this one's being strange.'

The wind swirled and the newcomer's scent insinuated itself into Gabble's nostrils. Gabble pawed it from his nose. Closer, now, the approaching shape was looking distinctly fluffy around the edges.

'Oh,' said Gabble. 'It's her.' He raised his voice and called out, 'What are you doing, Feather?'

The rat froze among the hedge thorns. It hesitated, as though deciding what to do. Then Feather stepped from her cover and pattered down to where Gabble and Ash were waiting.

She glowered at the pair of them. 'I,' she said primly, 'am feeding.'

Gabble ran a sceptical eye over her paws and whiskers. She didn't look or smell like a rat who had been eating. 'You're a long way from your burrow,' he said.

'So what?'

'So why feed right here?'

'Mind your own business.'

'Nice. Heh.'

'Gabble,' said Ash, pushing in front of him, 'is there any chance you could tell me who this is and what's going on?'

'This,' said Gabble, still watching Feather, 'is the Akla's daughter. She came to our naming. But I don't know why she's here now.'

Ash looked from Gabble to Feather. 'Our naming,' he repeated to himself. He opened his mouth to say something. But then a sound rang out, high and urgent, across the clanlands. Gabble's head snapped up. Next to him, Ash and Feather stiffened. An alarm. *Intruders. Help needed.*

'It's a call. We should go!' said Ash.

Feather nodded. 'We should. Come on.'

Gabble caught his brother's eye, which shone with excitement. But Ash was in no condition to fight.

'Ash—'

'Don't even think about telling me to stay here.'

Another call went up, now in several voices. *Intruders. Attack.*

Gabble dithered, split between his desire to help and his need to stop Ash from doing anything stupid. Feather gave him a disgusted look. 'Oh, pull yourself together,' she said. Then she ran, fur ruffling, for the source of the alarm.

Ash grinned after her. 'Ooh, she's making you look bad, Gabbley.' He gave Gabble a shove. 'Get going, will you? It's not like I can keep up anyway.'

Gabble nodded. Ash was right: any fight would be long over by the time he arrived. More calls, more urgent. And with a final glance at Ash, Gabble sprinted down the slope. He scrambled and tumbled down the hill to the main run, found his footing and ran swiftly on. He reached the junction where the runs split, and his paws turned him to the field, following its border to the increasing sound of conflict. He ducked beneath a tangle of bindweed and hurdled a tree root. Loose mud skittered out from beneath his paws, as he arrived, breathless, at the border tree. This place was the closest point to the Damplands, at the limit of the Greenhedge.

It was surrounded on one side by Notratlan and the other by the field. The tree's branches spread thickly overhead, and beneath them tall grasses gave way to bare, pocked earth and scattered leaves.

Gabble nosed between the grass stems, peeking cautiously into the clearing. The space was filled with the smell of pain and fear, and the sounds of scrabbling paws and coarse yells. He saw two rats dash up the far edge of the clearing, squeaking in distress and making for the Greenhedge. In the clearing itself six rats circled, two facing four. And nearer to Gabble a ratling was staggering, weaving an uncertain path towards him. He recognized Groom, a female from his side of the colony. He rushed to her side.

'Are you all right?'

On her coat he smelled anger and blood, and something else, fur-bristlingly sharp and foreign: the scent of another clan. She was bleeding from a bite on her back.

She tried to focus. 'Who—'

'It's me. Gabble. Are you all right?'

She pulled a face. 'Hurts. He needs help. Grist. And I saw Feather.'

'Find somewhere safe and wait,' said Gabble. 'I'll come back.' Then he ran for the nearest rats. As he came closer he recognized the bulk of Grist, up on his hind feet, boxing with a strange male. The fighters broke apart, sidling menacingly toward one another. Then the strange male caught sight of Gabble, and gave a short laugh.

'Reinforcements, is it?' he panted. 'Should I be surrendering? Or do I wait for your ratling to fight me?' The male's eyes remained fixed on Grist's face.

Grist glanced at Gabble, registered his presence. He smiled coldly. 'I'll spare you rolling over for Gabble. But only because you're such a nice rat.'

The male spat an insult and rushed forwards. Grist responded instantly, leaping and striking with his forepaws. The intruder was caught, half-turned. With a jarring collision both rats went down, sprawling and scrabbling on the earth. And then Grist was up, cleaning soil from his whiskers while the intruder gasped, winded. Grist caught Gabble's eye and winked.

'Damplanders,' he said by way of explanation. 'They haven't raided like this since I was a pup.' The male on the ground began clawing his way upright. 'I'd stay put if I were you,' Grist told him. He nodded to Gabble. 'I've got this one. Go and make yourself useful.' And as the other rat staggered to his feet, Grist lunged, biting for the Damplander's rump.

Gabble spun about, wild-eyed. Further down the clearing Feather, flanks heaving, was facing down three ratlings: a male and two females. She was bigger than any of them, and they advanced cautiously. As Gabble came to her side she whipped around, paws raised, and hair flying in all directions. He flinched back, instinctively raising his own paws. She blinked at him, nose and whiskers working.

'Oh, it's you,' she said. 'Finally.'

The male Damplander leapt for her, teeth bared.

'Feather!'

Feather spun back and boxed at the male's head, paws blurring. The male staggered sideways a few steps, and before he could right himself Feather jumped, landing squarely on his back. The two rats rolled over and over, squeaking and pummelling. Then they broke apart and the male cringed back. Feather shot Gabble a look.

'Do you want to try being helpful?' she demanded. Then she bared her teeth at the male, who fled. Feather sprinted after him. Gabble was left facing two rats: a female and a thin, young male. Both were lean, and their backs were arched, aggressively. They crept towards him, paw over paw. He watched carefully as they approached.

'Are you sure?' he called.

The female hesitated. 'What?'

'I said, are you sure? You know, that you want to attack me.'

She blinked.

'It hasn't gone too well for your friends, I think.' Gabble gestured at Feather's ratling who was in full flight, a determined Feather nipping at his haunches. 'You could get hurt. Or *I* could get hurt. Heh. And that would be much worse.'

The female stopped her advance, eyes narrowed. When Gabble made no movement she sat up. She cleaned her whiskers, thoughtfully, eyes fixed on Gabble's face. Her companion gave her an uncertain look and then he too stopped advancing.

'See, this is better, isn't it?' said Gabble, keeping his tone cheerful. 'Here we are and nobody's getting bitten.' He smiled at them. 'So you're Damplanders, then? That's nice. I've always wanted to meet one.'

The female nodded. Her expression said that she couldn't quite believe what was happening. *Which was fine*, thought Gabble. *Keep them guessing.*

'I'm Gabble,' he said. 'What's your name?'

And that, he knew later, was a mistake. There was a moment's outraged shock and then instant rage, lip curled, and ears flat.

'There are no names,' she spat. 'None but those we earn from the Taker.'

And she leapt for him. Gabble, taken by surprise, jumped away, but she caught him with her paws and the pair of them went down, grasping and striking. Gabble shoved at her and scrambled back as they broke apart. But the female was on him in an instant. He went over, paws up and struggling to hold her from him.

She clawed and snapped her teeth, almost hysterical in her attempts to hurt him. She lashed out, grabbing Gabble's belly fur, and dragged him closer. Gabble twisted aside and her teeth closed a mere fraction from his hind leg. The female came away with a mouthful of fur. In the moment's reprieve Gabble pulled his feet up to his belly and kicked out as hard as he could. The female flew backwards, landing in a tangle of limbs. But then she was up and breathing hard. She pawed a clump of hair from her mouth and glowered. Gabble glanced at his flank: a nasty-looking bald patch, and a little blood seeping through his skin.

'Heh. That's my fur,' he said.

The female, though, did not respond. She paced forwards, moving around to his left. To his right Gabble spied the male, sidling in a wide arc, cutting off the retreat. Gabble backed away, paw over paw, trying to watch both of them. If they attacked together he would lose. He raised his paws, facing the female. She was still tired from the fight, and the male was small. He could fight her first and perhaps deal with them singly. Maybe he could force them to retreat. He focused, blood racing, ready for the fight to begin. But then Gabble heard a thump and a squeak, and glanced over to see the male staggering away from Feather. The male tottered and fell to the ground, where he lay, dazed. Relief, so strong that Gabble could almost taste it. He turned to the female, a fierce smile on his face.

'Heh. I told you . . . fighting was a bad idea,' he panted.

The female glared. 'To die in the fight is no death,' she said.

Gabble frowned. Now what did *that* mean? But before he could reply, rustles broke out from the undergrowth.

At the far edge of the clearing, closest to the Damplands, rats were emerging from the grasses. Their smell spread thickly in the air as they gathered. They were Damplanders and they had come in numbers. And now Gabble saw triumph in the female's eyes. She ground her teeth at him. Part of Gabble was stunned, unable to believe that so many rats would come to the clanlands. The rest of him was thinking fast, searching the scenery for his clanmates, planning an escape. Groom was gone, and Grist was further up the clearing, alert and staring at the Damplanders. Silence descended as the rats from the two clans sized one another up. Nothing moved. *But soon*, Gabble thought, *soon we will have to run*. There were too many to fight, but Gabble felt his muscles clench with the desire to stay, to defend the clan. These were intruders. They didn't belong here.

A ripple of motion passed among the Damplanders. Gabble crouched, ready to flee. But then he realized that they weren't attacking. Instead they were jostling and gesturing towards the top of the clearing. The female in front of Gabble turned to see the source of their confusion. She blinked. Her eyes widened and a tremor ran through her body at the sight of something white that flashed among the grasses. A hacking, wheezing noise bubbled into the air, and a rat staggered into view, forging a slow but determined path out from amongst the stems. Gabble's chest tightened. It was Ash, and arriving at the worst possible moment. He saw Ash's whiskers twitch, and his head move from side to side, surveying the scene. Then he saw Ash grin.

'Well, now, this looks like fun.'

Then Ash convulsed, back arched and breath rasping. And when, finally, he had gasped his way upright, two red tears had trickled from his eyes. He pawed them from his face, smudging his fur. He blinked at the assembled rats. Gabble eyed the Damplanders nervously. But the female in front of him was trembling, right down to her tail tip. And the male who Grist had fought was gazing at Ash, mouth open. The eyes of every Damplander in the clearing were fixed, silently, on Ash.

'OK, this is weird. What's going on?' Then Ash spotted Gabble. 'Ah, Gabbley. That's good!' He tottered down the centre of the clearing, elbowing past Grist and making for where Gabble stood. He came to a stop and frowned at Gabble's disordered fur and new bald patch. 'Tsk. Gabble,' he said with mock disapproval, 'have you been fighting?'

'Not by choice. Heh,' said Gabble, giving the female a flat look.

'Still. Soon you'll be like a proper rat and everything.' He took in the stunned-looking female next to Gabble and then nodded at the other Damplanders. 'Who are all these, then?'

'Damplanders. And don't ask their names.'

Ash's face was alive with interest. 'Damplanders, eh?' He turned to the female, examining her curiously. She dropped her gaze. 'Whatzit, ratling,' said Ash. 'What brings you here?'

The female kept her eyes on the soil at her feet. Her jaw worked as though she wanted to speak, but she made no sound. She stole a glance at Ash, and then jerked her head back down.

'I—' she began. Then she shied back a few steps. Ash shot Gabble a puzzled look. The female saw his expression and pattered further back beyond reach.

'Hey, where are you going?' said Ash. He frowned as she flinched further away. 'Just stop, will you? I—'

The female fled. She sprinted down towards the waiting Damplanders. She raised her voice, calling out in a series of desperate squeaks something Gabble could not hear. But he could see her clanmates' shock and their fear. The female shot through their ranks, dashing away into the night. And they followed, forcing their way back through the grasses. As their rustles and squeaks receded, paws raced from behind Gabble and the final Damplander lurched past and disappeared into the darkness.

'Come back!' Ash yelled after him. He started after the fleeing rats, stumbling and wheezing as he went. 'Come back here and talk to me!'

But he could not keep up. By the time Ash's legs had carried him to the clearing's edge the Damplanders had gone.

'I'm not crazy.' Ash's voice was soft. His eyes, though, were hard. 'I'm not.'

Gabble tried again. 'No. I said *this* is crazy.' He picked his way hesitantly down the grass margin. 'And it is. Heh.'

Grist and Feather would have Groom safely back to the Greenhedge by now. The thought brought a tinge of guilt. Gabble had said he would go back for her. But Ash, of course, had other ideas. He had seen the others off with a wave of the paw, and a promise that he would follow. And then he had simply turned and started walking on his shaky legs, off in the direction the Damplanders had gone. His retreating form left Gabble with a choice: return to the burrow, or follow.

And now here they were, beyond the tree, and beyond the clanlands, forging a path down a thin strip of grass, caught between the blank stone of Notratlan on their right and the field on their left. But here the field grasses were gone, replaced by a vast, level plain of ripped and crumbled earth. Gabble knew with a cold certainty that this land was not for rats. The verge grasses bore a few smudges of scent, left recently by the Damplanders, but nothing more. And ahead the margin was littered with piles of rocks and odd, intricately jumbled metal shapes that rose up from roots part-buried in the soil. This was a strange, empty place, and the rising wind just made it stranger. The clouds moved quickly, smothering the world in darkness and revealing it in shafts of moonlight. Shadows ebbed and flowed over the ground and the night was alive with movement and ceaseless rustling. Gabble kept moving, trying not to think of what those rippling shadows might hold.

Ash's breath burbled as he staggered onward. Gabble watched him, tight-lipped. He had to get Ash back to the Greenhedge. If only he could find the right words then perhaps Ash would abandon this plan, return to the burrow, and give himself time to heal. Ash glanced over, and frowned.

'Don't give me that look. You saw how they reacted. I need to find those Damplanders. I need to know why.'

He laboured at the ground. His face was set, but his breath came in gasps and his legs shook with the effort. 'But you can head home. I don't need you here.'

'Right. So I'll go back and leave you here, shall I?' said Gabble. 'Heh. The Taker will find you.'

There was a sharp intake of breath. Ash stopped dead and wheeled to face Gabble. 'He already did,' Ash hissed.

Gabble felt his patience straining. 'For the Mother's sake, Ash, the Taker's just a story.'

'Story. Hah!' Ash gestured angrily at the stains on his face. 'Does this look like a story to you?'

'No, it looks like an ill rat who needs to rest,' Gabble returned. 'You say you saw the Taker, but that doesn't mean it happened. And it doesn't make this a good idea.'

Ash's eyes widened. And abruptly his anger was gone. 'You think I made it up?' The words were quiet, small. He placed a paw on Gabble's fur. 'Gabble, I wouldn't. Of all rats, I—' Ash's whiskers shook. He swallowed and looked away. 'I saw him. I did. And I thought at least you would believe me.'

'Ash—' Gabble began, cautiously.

'He gave me a name.' And now his eyes were hard again. Defiant.

'A name?'

'From his own lips.' Ash turned away. A strange

intensity had taken hold of his features. 'He whispered it to me. It was payment for what he took.'

'What he took? I don't understand.'

Something that could have been a laugh escaped Ash's lips. 'You mean you can't see?' Ash took his paw from Gabble's fur and gestured at his scrawny flanks. 'Look at me. This is what he took. He saw inside of me. He saw the rat that I wanted to be. He saw my future.' Ash's mouth twisted. 'And that's what he took.'

Gabble huddled down, tight against Ash's words. 'Heh. You need more time.'

'I've *had* time!' Ash shouted. 'I've eaten your Mother-forsaken grain and slugs. I've cringed beneath the hedge and pretended to be me.' Red tears rolled down Ash's cheeks. 'But it's an *act*. Can't you see that? I wanted to be a Bigrat. And now I can't even walk properly. He took *me* away, Gabble.' Ash thumped his chest. 'Me.'

Silence extended between them, broken only by Ash's breath and the rustling grasses. The rising wind ruffled their fur. And Gabble could think of nothing to say.

'What name?' he said finally.

Ash blinked. He looked up, with hope in his eyes.

'What name did the Taker give you?'

A smile crept onto Ash's lips. 'You believe me, then?'

And Gabble, left with little choice, nodded. 'Yes. All right, I do.'

Ash grasped him by the shoulders. 'Thank you.' Then he leaned forwards bringing his lips close to Gabble's ear. 'He called me Fo'dur, the Shining One.'

Gabbled pulled back, breaking Ash's grip. He stared at his brother in horror. *Oh, Mother, no.* Ash had taken his name. He opened his mouth to speak, unsure of what he was about to say. But then his eye caught a movement. A dark blur spilled from the shadows to their left. The night seemed to pool and surge forwards. A single thought shot through Gabble: cat!

Gabble slammed his forepaws into Ash's shoulder, sending his brother tumbling away. Then he leapt in the opposite direction. A colossal form plunged into the grasses where, an instant before, they had been standing. Its outstretched claws smacked into the ground, and Gabble was up and running in an instant. He pounded down the Notratlan border, hurdling stones and tearing through grasses, feet ripping at the ground. Dimly he heard a hacking noise, far behind, almost lost in the night. Ash. Gabble swerved madly into the lee of a pile of square-edged rocks, and huddled there, listening. He could hear only the wind, drowning out even his own rapid breathing. But that gave Gabble hope. If Ash had found cover then the breeze might mask his scent and sound. There might still be a chance.

Gabble grabbed for the nearest rock and hauled and scrabbled his way up the pile. Fragments tumbled from beneath his feet, but in moments he had gained the top. He crouched low, exposed in the Taker's moon and buffeted by the wind, and stared back the way he had come. The verge was a patchwork of shadows, muddling in the breeze. They surged and retreated, playing amidst the rippling grass. To his left Notratlan stared emptily back, its stone and shadows unmoving, and at his right lay the broken field. Gabble dismissed them, concentrating on the verge. That's where Ash would be, in a small, dark refuge. There: at the very edge of Notratlan from the gloom beneath a tussock, the shade held the merest suggestion of a lighter patch. Gabble watched it until he was certain, and his heart began to race. It was Ash, he was sure of it. The breeze whipped up a cloud of dust that twirled from Notratlan and into Gabble's face. He narrowed his eyes against it, and turned his head away. And as he did, he saw a movement in the field, and a flash of yellow-green eyeshine. The cat was padding towards Ash's hiding place.

Gabble closed his eyes. What could he do? From nowhere a memory arrived. Their time in Notratlan, Shrill, the ratling, and his threats. *I call the cat on you.* Gabble's eyes snapped open. *Call the cat. Not good, not good.* But his body stood up on its hind legs and swayed in the breeze. And up on his pile of rocks, he raised his chin. *Mother protect me*, he thought.

'Hey, ugly!' he yelled. 'Hey, this way!'

He jumped up and down, squeaking. And in the distance, the slick, black patch paused.

'That's right, I'm talking to you! Who do you think you are, hunting sick rats? Heh? Come and hunt me. I'll give you a run!'

Eyes shone out of the darkness. They fixed on his position. Then they vanished. A flurry of movement and the cat was gone. Gabble froze. Had it seen him? Was it coming? Or was it still tracking Ash? He raked the landscape, seeking the predator. But the shifting moonlight and swirling scent made it impossible.

A rustle ahead and to his right. Gabble's head jerked to follow it. Nothing. He crouched, ears, nose, and whiskers twitching. Wind, dust, moon, breathing, heart, blood. Eyes and ears to watch the front, scent from behind. He shifted, trying to keep the wind at his back, but it danced around. It brought a snatch of cat-scent, evil in his nostrils. He heard a tiny clinking sound and turned to it . . . and stopped breathing. Notratlan was gone, blotted by greyness that resolved into a claw, spike-tipped, outstretched, just beyond striking distance. And behind the claw, yellow eyes, pupils wide and fixed hungrily on him.

With a single, panicked squeak Gabble was down the rocks, on the grass and running for his life. Behind him stones slid and toppled, and paws thudded to the ground. A low growl and the cat was after him. Terror, muscles and paws, and whiskers that flicked against grasses as he bolted down the verge, away from Ash and the clanlands. A sense of movement behind and Gabble dodged. Claws lashed and he leapt left, then scrabbled right as the cat pounced again, landed badly, mewed in frustration. For an instant the cat sprawled, and distance opened between them. But then the ground beat again to the sound of pursuit. Spurred on, Gabble raced, head up, seeking shelter. Nothing, nothing. Then there, on the Notratlan border, a frame of tangled metal lurched into view. Gabble, almost sobbing, wrenched his body around and hurtled for it, breath raw in his throat. The frame's base was lost in choking grass, no gap, no shelter. But, almost invisible in the pattern of the structure, Gabble spied a hole, a mere rat-width across. He dived for it. He grabbed at the metal and clawed and battled at the plants that twined through it. His head and shoulders thrust through, squirmed clear. But his haunches jammed. The ghost of imagined claws swiped for him with back-breaking strength. He fought, raking and shoving, dragging and squeaking. And, with a final heave, the metal released him and Gabble tumbled, face first into darkness. A moment to lie panting then up, up on quivering limbs. He turned his paws and whiskers to the metal, scanning the space and seeking openings.

His frantic search found nothing but a gap at the soil surface, enough to permit moonglow, but not a cat's paw. Night air wafted in, cooling Gabble's fur as he slumped, shuddering with exhaustion, against the frame. *Safe. Thank the Hunter.*

Paws stepped softly up to the metal cage. Gabble rolled to his feet and backed as far from the sound as he could. A dark shape moved behind the rat-hole, and warm breath poured cat stench into the space. The cat growled, a low sound, feral and visceral. Then it moved away, padding through the grass and around to the far side. The moonglow was snuffed as it crouched. More breath steamed through the frame. A paw clouted the metal, then withdrew. Gabble huddled, barely breathing, as the cat circled, now clawing, now sniffing for gaps. But it found no way in. It climbed on top of the pile. The frame sagged, with a little rasping sound, and clinks and tinkles as pebbles and soil rained down. But the structure held. The cat jumped down. It tracked once more around the outside then gave one final sniff and stalked away, to be lost in the grass.

chapter seven

How long Gabble waited he did not know, but the moon had begun to set by the time he dared ease himself out. He squeezed beneath the low exit and checked carefully before pulling himself into the open. Then he breathed out, faint with relief. He groomed his fur straight, wincing at the bald patch the Damplander had given him, and wiped the cat smell from his whiskers. He listened again, just to be sure. Only then did he allow himself a small smile. In front of him Notratlan gleamed in the moonlight's dregs. Across its surface a distant wall rose, one side of the henburrow. The wind now slanted steadily across the stone, bringing hints of dust, rock, straw and chicken. Gabble faced back up the verge. Ash would be there somewhere. If he had any brain he would be heading home. Heh, which meant that he would still be coming this way. Gabble's jaw set. He was going to force Ash back to the Greenhedge if he had to roll him there like an egg.

He stepped away from the frame, ready to set off up the verge. He scented the air and scanned the grasses for the best route . . .

. . . and froze. As his head came around, behind him, right at the edge of vision, he caught a movement. He barely breathed. He turned his neck, just enough to see black belly fur brushing grasses that bent stealthily aside. It was right behind him, no more than a rat's length away. Realization chilled to his paws. The cat had not gone. It had never gone. It had out-waited him, downwind and out of sight. And he hadn't seen it.

Gabble trembled as the beast closed on him. His leg twitched, but he forced it to stillness. He couldn't run. If he moved too soon the cat would snap out his life. He had only one chance: to wait for it to leap. Then he might take it by surprise. As slowly as he could Gabble eased himself into a crouch, keeping the predator at the very edge of his vision. The cat placed a forepaw, transferred its weight. The second paw drew up. The cat's eyes never left Gabble's back. It brought up its rear feet without a sound. The wind bore its scent away. It had been clever. If Gabble hadn't looked around he would never have seen it. *Stop thinking, now.*

Concentrate. Be ready. Gabble crouched as low as he could, every muscle ready to spring. The cat crouched too. *Wait.*

Wait.

The cat leapt. Gabble hurled himself forwards. He heard a surprised mew as its claws met with air, and Gabble was away, sprinting for Notratlan. His paws jarred on stone that sped beneath him. The cat was up and flowing in an instant. And now Gabble was running towards nothing but wall. No protection, no metal frame this time to save him. He ran through ragged muscles, burning paws, and aching lungs. He ran in the sheer hope that anyone—the Hunter, Taker, Mother, or Trickster—could see him, would help him. He smacked against the henburrow, and yanked his body around. A paw snapped down, blocking his way. He whirled but a second paw blurred, slamming into the stone a hair from his nose. Trapped, with paws to each side, Gabble faced his attacker. The cat's head filled his whole world: whiskers, teeth, tongue, and eyes with pupils narrowing. Gabble watched its shoulders and forelegs bunch, and claws slide from their sheaths then back again. *It was ready*, he thought. *Ready to end his life.*

Yelling with defiance, Gabble leapt to the attack. He flung himself at the cat, but a paw lashed, and battered him aside. He sprawled, then gasped as a colossal weight shot down onto his back. It ground between his shoulders, and his chin smacked against the ground. He wriggled beneath the cat's weight, his hind legs flailing, kicking out dust and stones. But he found no purchase. His forepaws splayed uselessly out in front of him. Crushed between the paw on his back and the rock at his chest, he couldn't breathe. He tried to twist, to yank his body around, anything to bring his legs and teeth to bear. But then the cat unsheathed its claws. They speared into Gabble's flesh, hooking down through his skin.

Gabble went utterly still.

The cat dragged him back towards its mouth. Gabble squeaked with pain as his belly and paws skittered across the ground. Then it stopped and moist breath ruffled his fur. It released its grip for an instant, enough for hope. Gabble shoved his legs straight, but the weight snapped back, crushing him once more. Air rushed from his lungs. He tried to breathe in, but could not. All of his strength could not shift the weight, nor draw air into his starving chest.

Gabble's eyes closed and his body went limp. Strange. He should be terrified, but now it seemed that his body and he were two different things. The cat, keeping Gabble's shoulders pinned, batted at his haunches, twisting them. Gabble heard a cry of pain, and knew it had come from his mouth. But that was only the last dregs leaving his lungs. He felt nothing. The hurt and the fear were happening to a Gabble who was somehow distant. Somewhere else, but also here, was a rat with a true name, called Fo'dur. This rat had saved his brother from death. He had earned his pride. And perhaps he would meet the Taker. Maybe he could ask him to give Ash his life back. Maybe not. But Ash was safe. That mattered. What happened to Gabble, somehow did not. Gabble would end here. But Fo'dur still had places to go, places without pain, and which lay far beyond Notratlan.

A loud squeak rang across the stone and echoed from the wall. The cat jerked upright, startled. It stared away, eyes wide, to the source of the sound. The force that pinned Gabble lifted, fractionally. Air rushed into his body. His eyes snapped open, and his lethargy disappeared, replaced by a surge of anger. He twisted and kicked, ignoring the tearing of claws in his skin. The cat's head came around and its mouth opened. But too late. Gabble was on his back, and his neck and forepaws were free. He grabbed for the pinioning claw, dragged it to his face then sank his teeth deeply into it, tasting fur and blood.

The cat threw back its head and screamed. It yanked its paw away, mewling with hurt. Gabble twisted up, lunging for the cat's other forepaw, snapping at it. The cat leapt aside, stumbling in its haste to escape the attacking rat. Gabble squeaked in pure rage, lunging again. The cat pedalled backward, eyes wide with alarm.

Gabble stood up, paws raised, facing down the cat and panting. The cat made a hesitant movement, and Gabble snapped his teeth and squeaked at it. The cat placed its wounded paw gingerly on the ground, and then picked it back up with a hiss. It licked at the paw, with a mournful expression.

And Gabble filled with a savage joy. 'Heh,' he panted. His back felt raw and bruised. His ribs hurt. But he drew himself up, trembling and ready to leap. 'You don't like it, do you? You don't like it when it hurts.'

The same, piercing cry came again from the verge. Gabble saw the barest flicker of uncertainty on the cat's face. It cocked an ear and half-turned to the sound. And that was enough. Gabble hurled himself forwards once more, biting and squeaking. His senses filled with the acrid taste of cat and his own yells were joined by a roar from the cat as it wrenched up its paw, sending Gabble spinning away.

He landed in a heap against the wall. He coughed, and scrabbled at the ground, trying to clear his head, to come back to his feet. *He must move. He must.* He dragged at the ground, desperate to regain his feet. He raised his head, wincing, expecting the teeth or claws that would send him to the Taker. But instead the cat sat a short distance away, licking at its paw. Gabble stood, carefully, eyes fixed on his enemy. They faced one another for long moments. Then the cat stood and slowly placed its paw on the ground. The strange call came a final time. The cat flinched and its injured paw buckled beneath it. It gave a plaintive cry, and whisked the paw from the ground. Then it turned and limped away. It rounded the corner of the henburrow and disappeared from view.

Gabble staggered off in the opposite direction, up the wall towards the henburrow door. The world spun, sickeningly, as he reached it, but clinging to the wood helped. Then he slipped into the musty world of chickens and rats within. Not a hen stirred from the perches above as his paws took him along the walls, following the scents of the rats who lived there.

He found himself slumping against the wall. Strange. He had just been walking. It took an effort to get back to his feet. A patter broke out from the darkness and by the time he had regained his balance, rats were standing in front of him. He recognized the scent of Ar'bus, the big scarred male who had fought Ash. He caught snatches of whispers. Ar'bus's voice and the female. Snip.

'. . . wrong with his back.'

'. . . why we should help, he's a . . .'

And from behind him came the approach of another rat. High-pitched squeaking filled the air, with voices raised in argument. He didn't care. His back hurt. He reached a paw around. It came back wet, and stained red.

'Heh. This . . . this isn't good for rats.' Gabble's legs wobbled. It took a force of will to stop them from collapsing under him. 'Need . . .' Gabble shook his head to clear it. But it had become heavy. He could not lift it properly and the movement made him stagger.

'. . . . sleep,' he said.

And the world jumbled. More shouting, then quiet, and urgent paws and whiskers, a sense of being lifted, dragged, and then something soft and warm and a darkness that flowed across him. It entered his mind and swept his thoughts to a strange, distant place.

'There's water there, lad. Best you drink it.'

Gabble moaned. The heavy absence that had settled on him eased away. It took a moment to place who had spoken. Ar'bus. That was the name. A paw at his shoulder rocked him again.

'Drink, youngling. I've seen rats die for want of water.'

Gabble opened his eyes blearily. Moonlight stung them, leaking through the boards that made up the wall of this nest. Nearby, water dripped, pooling in a hollow in the floor. Gabble's tongue was thick. He was thirsty. He tried to stand, and could not. He was tempted to simply lie back down and let sleep claim him. But he forced his legs to straighten, wincing as his muscles stiffened and pulled. He tottered to the water and drew it down in deep gulps.

'You've lost fur, skin, and some blood,' Ar'bus continued, watching him. 'You were lucky not to lose more than that.'

Gabble only half listened. He drank the water, enjoying how it salved the rawness of his throat. Then he twisted with a grimace to see his injuries. Scabbed. Ugly. But it meant he was healing.

'Lucky. Heh,' said Gabble, and went back to drinking.

'You took on a cat and you're breathing,' said Ar'bus. 'That's as lucky as there is.' He snorted. 'Cat-baiting. And I thought you were the clever one.'

Gabble stopped drinking and staggered around to face the older rat.

'I don't feel clever,' Gabble told him. 'Ash. My brother. Did you see him?'

Ar'bus shook his head. 'No. Sorry, lad.'

Gabble closed his eyes. 'How long have I been here?'

'The rest of that night and all day. The moon is new risen.'

Gabble nodded. 'I see.' That was a long time. Anything could have happened to Ash. He might still be out there. He could be lost or worse.

Gabble drank again, then raised his head. The last drops ran down the fur of his chin.

'You didn't have to help me,' he said. 'Thank you. I owe you a debt. My name's Gabble.'

'Well, Gabble,' said Ar'bus, leaning forwards 'I'll take that debt. But if I'm as honest as a rat should be, I'll admit that I was tempted to leave you. You said you wouldn't come back.'

'I didn't have the choice,' said Gabble. He drank once more, a few final gulps. 'So why did you help me?'

Ar'bus gave a short bark of a laugh. 'You have the young female to thank for that.' Something like a smile tugged at the hard lines of his mouth. 'She was . . . insistent. You'll have to ask her why yourself. Can you walk?'

Gabble nodded.

'Best you come with me, then.'

Ar'bus set off out of the dusty chamber, and Gabble followed. He felt light. His muscles ached and the scabs on his back pulled, but movement made things better. The solid coldness of the stone beneath his paws brought him back, and the smells of rats and chickens were real in his senses. Hunger began to ache in his belly. Ar'bus led him out from under cover, and they scampered across a dark corner of the henburrow. Gabble kept an eye on the roosts above, but the noise from the birds was all broody contentment. They followed the wall a short distance, and then slipped through a hole into cosy, rat-scented passages that delved deep into a vast stack of dried grasses. The hen noises receded as they wound further into the stack, following the scents to the main burrow.

They came out into a chamber in which Snip and Shrill were grooming. Snip nodded to him, and carried on washing her ears. Shrill paused mid-scratch, then glowered and ground his teeth at Gabble. He disappeared off down a tunnel.

'He's upset because you hurt his cat,' said Ar'bus, watching him go. 'He'll get over it.'

Gabble surveyed the chamber. It was small, but warm and homely. *So this was what lay beyond Notratlan*, he thought. Maybe it wasn't so bad after all. The scents here were strange, though. The nose-wrinkling wrongness of a different clan's scent was all around. Unthinkingly he raised his paws to wash it away. But then he dropped them. He was the intruder, here, and he shouldn't call attention to it. He turned to find Ar'bus watching him with an unreadable expression.

'Food,' said Ar'bus, gesturing at a small pile of grain. Gabble limped towards it, but then paused.

'You said a young female.'

Snip stopped grooming. 'Ah, yes,' she said. She smiled at Gabble's perplexed expression. 'Just a moment.' And she scurried off down a tunnel. Gabble heard

115

muted speech, and the sound of feet approaching. Snip pattered back into the room, looking amused, and moved to block the chamber's exit. And a moment later Feather stomped into view. She stood at the threshold, scowling at the assembled rats. Then she saw Gabble. Her gaze settled on his torn back, and his fur plastered with scabs and the scowl dropped from her face. She reached out a paw, gently, as if to touch him. Then she glanced at the rats around her and scowled again.

Snip sighed. 'Quite a friend you have there,' she said to Gabble. 'She kept fighting until we promised to help you.' She winced at the memory. 'Since then she's been sitting in there refusing to talk.'

'Ah,' said Gabble. 'I see.' But he didn't. Not really. Feather was here. That was probably odd, but all he could think about was how hungry he was. He picked up some grain and chewed it from its husk. He swallowed and grabbed for the next.

'Here's a mess,' said Ar'bus, shaking his head at Snip. 'We have two Hunters: one who says he owes us a debt and one who won't talk. Question is, what do we do with them?'

'A debt, is it?' Unexpectedly Snip broke into peals of laughter. 'Who'd have thought it, a debt from a Hunter,' she said. Then she regarded Gabble closely, eyes narrowed. 'But this one's no Hunter. Not really. He has too much of the Trickster in him.'

'What are you talking about?' Feather demanded. 'We're not Hunters or anything else. We're from the Greenhedge. Can't you see that? And you,' she said, turning to Gabble, 'are in a lot of trouble. What in the name of the Mother do you think you're doing here? And who are all these rats anyway?'

'Oh, *now* she talks,' Snip muttered.

Ar'bus frowned at Feather. 'Doesn't matter where you're from, lass. It's who you follow that counts.'

Feather met Ar'bus's gaze with a haughty stare. Gabble swallowed his mouthful. 'I don't follow the Hunter,' he said.

'No.' said Snip, eyes twinkling. 'That's what I said. But your Akla does, doesn't he?'

'I don't know,' said Gabble, still chewing. 'Sorry.'

Ar'bus turned an eye to Snip. 'Like I told you, the Greenhedge has forgotten its stories.' Then he faced Gabble and Feather. 'It's the oldest tale. You'll have heard it from your Mothers. Did you never think what it meant?'

Gabble, paws and mouth full of grain, shook his head. The oldest tale was just a story, a part of his puphood, like the walls of his burrow or the Mothers' soft voices.

'We all have choices to make and tunnels to tread,' said Snip. 'The seeds of those choices lie deep in the stories, and the oldest tale carries the deepest seed. I'll tell you the story, and then we'll work out what to do with you.'

'I don't think—' Feather began, but Snip cut her off.

'He's feeding, and you have time,' said Snip. 'Why not listen? Perhaps you might see the world differently.'

Feather glanced at Gabble, but he, thoughts clouded, simply nodded and carried on eating. Feather retreated to the burrow wall and settled down, looking sullen. Snip began speaking into the still henburrow air.

'Before there were names there was the Mother. She was the first, and she was of the earth. She nested in her chambers, deep in the belly of the world. It was there that three brothers came to her, seeking their names. The first was a strong rat, quick and bold. She named him Ca'thir, the Hunter, and gave him a piece of her heart. "If my children follow you," she told him, "they shall hunt, and grow strong."

'The second was a slight rat. He was full of laughter, dancing, and wit. This rat she named Ta'klar, the Trickster. To him too she gave a piece of her heart, with the words, "If my children follow you they will have words and wits and the love of dancing." '

'We know the story,' said Feather, coldly. 'But I don't see—'

'That's because you speak when you shouldn't,' said Ar'bus, roughly. The scars on his face twisted as he spoke. Feather quickly closed her mouth.

118

'Hush, ratling,' said Snip. She stepped forwards and laid a paw on Ar'bus, who subsided with a grunt. 'Now the third brother was a silent rat, bone-white and red-eyed. To him the Mother bowed her head. "My lonely friend," she said, "your name is Ra'lg, but I cannot give you my heart." And red tears crept from her eyes as she spoke. "For you are the Taker, who is there when strength fails and the dance ends. My children will come to you, and you must guide them to the world beyond." '

Gabble dropped the last husks and groomed dust from his muzzle. He frowned, turning his thoughts to the story. Every pup, ratling, and Bigrat knew this tale. But here, told by this strange rat, its meaning seemed to twist.

Snip continued, 'The Taker cried out that his brothers now had hearts to share, and why should he alone remain heartless? To this the Mother replied, "My heart will come to you in the children you guide. And so, one day, you too shall have it for your own." And then she sent him to the Land of Bones, at the threshold of the world beyond, where he remains to this day. And the Mother returned to her deepest chambers in the belly of the earth, never again to leave them. The Trickster and Hunter, bearing their names but bereft of their brother, walked out to live in the wide world.'

'And so it is,' said Ar'bus, from his position at the burrow wall, 'that we are each born with a fragment of the Mother's heart, and we carry it to the Taker. The rats we follow, the Hunter and Trickster, grant us names, as a sign to their brother that we are worthy. These names we keep safe within us, with our piece of the Mother's heart. And when we are done we give them to the Taker, and he guides us to the world beyond. And at the end of all things, when night no longer comes and the earth crumbles beneath us, the Taker will at last have a full heart of his own, made from the names of every true rat he guides. So the story goes.' He gave Gabble a level look. 'The rest I'm sure you know.'

Gabble nodded. *And so love the Mother, run with the Hunter, and dance with the Trickster. But keep a place, deep and safe, and fill it with your name. For one day you will meet the Taker in his Land of Bones. And it is best to be ready.*

Snip had been watching Gabble's face, and now a wry smile twitched in her whiskers. 'Ah. I think our clever one begins to understand.'

'Maybe,' said Gabble. 'It's not only about names. I think it's also about clans.'

'Clans,' Ar'bus grunted. 'Once, perhaps, when rats knew themselves. Once, when we honoured those who lived their names.' He shook his head. 'But not now. The oldest tale has lost its meaning. You seek your name from the Hunter, because this is what your Akla expects, because it's good for your clan. But if you earn it, what then? Will you live it as you should?' Ar'bus leaned in towards Gabble and tapped his chest. 'In here each of us carries a heart and our name. Clan or no clan, we must keep them pure for the Taker.'

Feather made a disgusted sound and huddled down further into her fur. But something in Ar'bus's words nagged at Gabble, right at the edge of understanding. *May the Hunter guide you.* That's what Grist had said before he had name raided. And Gabble had earned his name by hunting, hadn't he? But new thoughts nagged at him, things he had never considered. *This one's no Hunter. He has too much of the Trickster in him.* Why would Snip have said that? And what did Ar'bus believe? Or the Damplanders?

'Damplanders.' Gabble realized he had spoken the word aloud. Ar'bus and Snip were looking at him. Gabble met their gaze. 'Who do they follow?'

'They say they follow the Taker,' said Snip.

Ar'bus spat. 'They have no name, and no honour. They follow death. Nothing more.'

There are no names, Gabble thought. That's what the Damplander female had said to him when they fought. *None but those we earn from the Taker.* Her words still

121

made little sense, and there was something else, here, something that if he just thought for a moment . . .

A call echoed out around the henburrow. Ar'bus and Snip came instantly alert.

'Shrill,' said Snip. 'He's found something.'

'Snip, keep her here,' Ar'bus ordered, gesturing at Feather. 'I'll have to take this one with me.' He turned a narrow look on Gabble. 'Come with me, lad, but keep your mouth shut and paws to yourself. Any trouble and there will be consequences. Understood?'

Gabble nodded.

'Very well.' Ar'bus nodded to Snip and pattered quickly from the chamber. Gabble gave Feather a final look, hoping she wouldn't do anything violent. Then he followed Ar'bus, moving as quickly as he could with his injured back.

'What is it?' he asked.

'Damplander, most likely,' Ar'bus grunted. 'They think Notratlan is deadly. Mainly because we make sure they never go back to tell of us.'

Ar'bus's voice was hard. Gabble kept his paws moving, grateful that he couldn't see the expression on the older rat's face.

chapter eight

The fight was over by the time they arrived. They followed Shrill's calls to a disused corner of the henburrow, away from the main chamber with its chickens. Here the Notratlan walls still stretched above them, but Shrill's trail ducked beneath sheets of close-fitting wood, supported by a series of broad, wooden tunnels. He had chased a ratling into one of these and corralled it at the end, imprisoned by wood, with stone at its back. Gabble could hear its panicked breathing, and the scrabble of its paws as they searched the walls for an escape.

'It's a Damplander, Ar'bus,' said Shrill, as they approached. 'I calls the cat on it, but the cat don't come.' These last words were accompanied by a furious glare for Gabble. 'So I chases it here like you says I should.'

'Good rat, Shrill,' said Ar'bus. 'Now go and take over from Snip. I'll need her here.'

Shrill stepped aside, fur still bristling, allowing Ar'bus to pass. Then he shouldered past Gabble and scampered away.

'He's a willing lad, but you hurt his cat,' said Ar'bus. 'Best he's gone for a bit.'

Gabble nodded and Ar'bus turned his attention back to the cornered Damplander—who shrank back still further.

'They're not so brave when it's just one of them,' said Ar'bus. There was something in his expression that sent a chill through Gabble. 'And we make sure it's never more than one that comes.'

Gabble saw the ratling register Ar'bus's words. He heard its despairing squeak. It rushed forwards, pawing at Ar'bus in a bid for freedom. Ar'bus met it with smooth force, clouting it to the floor at Gabble's feet. Gabble caught a snatched impression of its rolling eyes and terrified scent before Ar'bus grabbed it by the fur and pinned it, just as he had with Ash. Gabble drew down more scent: fear, defiance, and the smell of the Damplanders' clan. But beneath that lay something familiar, as though he had met this rat before. But that was impossible, wasn't it?

The ratling squeaked again. Words spilled from Gabble's mouth.

'Stop it!' he cried. 'She's frightened.'

Ar'bus's head snapped around with a glare. 'I told you to keep out of it. This isn't your place.'

'I know. But please listen,' said Gabble. 'There's something you're missing here. I've met this Damplander before.'

In Ar'bus's instant of hesitation the female ratling began clawing at the ground. He tightened his grip and her struggles stopped.

'She's a Damplander,' Ar'bus rasped. 'Their sort must learn.'

Beneath Ar'bus's weight the female ratling was frozen with fear. The only movement was her quick, distressed breathing and the panicked movements of her eye. But Gabble knew her, now. She was the female he had fought in the clearing, days—was it days?— before. But why was she here? He studied her for a moment.

Then he chuckled. The sound struck an odd note, but Gabble couldn't help it. 'Learn,' he repeated, turning a bright eye to Ar'bus. 'Well. Heh. I'm sure she's learned a lot already. I mean she already thinks it wasn't a good idea to come here.'

Ar'bus growled low in his throat. 'I warn you—' Ar'bus began, but Gabble cut him off.

'Let me speak with her,' Gabble insisted. 'Please.'

'And then what? Leave her to fetch other

Damplanders?' Ar'bus shook his head. 'Do you reckon we can fight the whole Damplander clan?'

'No,' said Gabble. 'But there's nothing to be lost in talking, I think.'

Gabble heard Snip arrive behind him.

'Oh, let him talk, Ar'bus,' she said. 'He obviously wants to, and he's asking so nicely.'

'Very well,' Ar'bus muttered. But he did not relax his grip on the Damplander.

'Thank you,' said Gabble. Then he pattered closer to where the female lay. He ignored Snip's quiet laugh and the words, *so polite*, beneath her breath. 'Hello,' he said to the ratling, 'my name's Gabble. I told you that last time but you weren't impressed. Heh.'

She watched him, beadily, from beneath Ar'bus's weight. He thought he saw a glimmer of recognition in her eyes.

'They tell me I'm a Hunter or something,' Gabble continued. 'Or I might not be any more. Anyway, I'm here because my brother's an idiot and I can't run faster than a cat. Who are you?'

The female's eyes closed.

'I am one with no name,' she said. Gabble's heart sank. She wasn't helping. 'One who wishes to die in the fight.'

Ar'bus made a contemptuous noise. 'You see, lad? We're doing her a favour.'

Gabble did not answer, his attention on the ratling. 'Die in the fight, eh?' he said. 'Sounds nasty, that. But you're breathing now and you don't look like you want to stop. I think you *really* want Ar'bus to get off and leave you alone.' Gabble took a step forwards, bringing his face closer to hers. 'Would you like Ar'bus to get off and leave you alone?'

'Who says I'll do that?'

'Just ignore him and answer the question,' said Gabble, giving the ratling a friendly wink. 'He's like this with new people. Heh.'

The female stared as if she thought Gabble was insane. Then she craned her neck around and gazed up into Ar'bus's scarred, fierce face. Her mouth opened. 'Yes. All right?' she said. 'Yes, I want him to get off me. Is that what you want to hear?'

'Yes,' said Gabble, giving her an encouraging smile. 'That's what I want to hear. Ar'bus, can you let her up?'

He had pushed his luck too far. Ar'bus's face twisted into a snarl. 'Gabble, you anger me. You are here on sufferance.'

'There's nothing to lose,' Gabble insisted. 'She can't go far.'

Ar'bus glowered for long moments. Then, moving with deliberate slowness, he settled back, allowing the ratling to her feet. But he kept his body between her and the exit. Released, she leapt up and scampered back to the wall, glaring balefully out at the other rats.

Ar'bus's lip curled. 'You have what you wished for. Talk fast.'

'Talk fast,' Gabbled repeated. 'Heh. Now that I'm good at.' He pattered down the tunnel towards the Damplander ratling. She rose up on her hind paws, uncertain of his intention. Gabble stopped short.

'You don't really want to die, do you?' he asked, softly. Despite what you said.'

The female hesitated, then shook her head.

'I don't want you to either. I can help, I think. I have some ideas in my head, and you need to tell me if they're right or wrong. Can you do that?'

The female nodded. Gabble could feel Ar'bus's gaze on the pair of them. Half-formed ideas of names and Hunters and Takers swirled in his mind. He closed his eyes. Time to let the words come.

'I think . . .' said Gabble. 'I think you didn't want to come here. Not really.'

For a long, horrible, moment the female did not speak. But then she said. 'No. I didn't.'

'But you had to?'

A nod.

Eyes closed, the memories and thoughts flowed. This female in the clearing, and her sudden attack when he had asked her name.

'You came for a name.'

'Yes.'

'And that's why you came to my clan and fought me. For a name. It was a name raid.' The words passed from thought to air, and he was certain they were right. The right words at the right time. His gift. 'But it went wrong. Because you saw Ash and you ran away.'

He opened his eyes, caught the expression on her face: fear, and shame.

'A—Ash?'

'The white rat,' said Gabble.

The female flinched. 'The Taker,' she breathed.

Gabble stared. 'The Taker? You think Ash is the Taker?'

She shook her head. But he could see fear in her eyes. It didn't make sense. If she didn't think he was the Taker, what was she scared of?

'He came to us,' she said, 'the white one. Just like Rai'thir said. He told us about the rats and eggs, and I thought . . .' Her voice quavered, and she swallowed, quickly.

Gabble gaped. A confusion of thoughts and emotions swamped him, a mixture of joy and disbelief. Ash was alive. She had said so. But she also said that Ash was with the Damplanders.

He spoke, and the words came out sharp. 'Ash went to the Damplanders? He told you about Notratlan?'

She flinched but nodded. Gabble closed his eyes against a twist of grief. *Oh, Ash. You idiot.* Gabble turned to face Ar'bus, and saw a reflection of his thoughts in the older rat's face. The Damplanders were kept from Notratlan by fear. That's what Ar'bus said. And if this female was right then Ash had told them of Ar'bus, Snip, and Shrill. He had told them that there were rats to fight and eggs to be had.

The female looked from Gabble to Ar'bus. She raised her head. 'So, there. I've answered your questions. Now release me or let me die in the fight. I am ready.'

Ready to die, Gabble thought. *But also scared.*

And a moment later the female's head went down again. 'All I wanted was my name,' she said, miserably. 'It's not fair.'

Gabble studied her. *My name.* And an idea popped into his mind.

'Your mother,' he said. 'What did she call you?'

The breath hissed between the female's teeth. 'There are no names—'

'—but those you earn from the Taker. Yes, you said that. So you have no name, then? Nothing that rats can call you?'

The female shook her head. But Gabble, who was watching carefully, caught her hesitation, and the way she avoided his gaze. And then he knew he was right. He opened his paws to her, in something like

130

supplication. 'My mothers called me Gabble. It's just my pupname, but I think it matters.' He smiled. 'Gabble. I always thought they did it for a joke, because I spoke strangely when I was a pup. My brother says I still do. Heh. But sometimes, when I need them, the right words come. It's like I grew to fit my name, or it shaped me, somehow. And I think . . . I think that maybe the name wasn't really a joke at all.'

The female was watching him, her expression unreadable.

'It was their wish for me,' said Gabble. 'That one day I would speak well. It was there for me to grow into, so I could be ready for my true name. And so I wonder,' Gabble continued, softly, 'I just wonder what it was that your mother wished for you. What name did she whisper to you, in the nest where nobody else could hear?'

When the female next spoke her voice was no more than a whisper. 'Hope,' she said. 'She called me Hope.'

And she began to cry. Gabble hung his head. This was no Damplander. This was a young, frightened ratling, stranded and alone amongst strangers. And if he had been a Damplander, rather than from the Greenhedge, he too would be where she was, crying for a lost life. He wanted to comfort her, and tell her that everything would be all right. But these things were not his to promise.

'Hope,' he said. 'That's a wonderful name.' He turned and looked into Ar'bus's face. 'So what will you do?' he asked. 'Will you grant a mother's wish?'

Ar'bus met Gabble's gaze and held it for an instant. He glanced at Snip, who looked away.

'All right, curse you,' Ar'bus growled. He jerked his head at Hope. 'You. You go.'

Hope's head came up, eyes bright with disbelief.

'I said go,' said Ar'bus. 'Now, before I change my mind.'

Hope took a tentative step forwards. Then she bolted for the entrance, shoving past Gabble, Ar'bus, and Snip. The sound of her paws, on wood and stone, faded into the night.

'A Damplander's freedom,' said Ar'bus. He snorted. 'May it give her what she wishes.' He turned to Gabble. 'Hope has gone, Gabble. You and your brother have seen to that. And soon she'll bring the Damplanders here. What now for us, do you think?'

Ar'bus turned away, and began to walk, wearily back up the tunnel. Snip turned to follow but then paused and studied Gabble's face. 'There's something about you,' she said at last. 'You're different. I don't know what you are because you haven't decided. Not yet.' There was no laughter in her voice as she spoke, and her eyes were fixed on Gabble's. 'I trust your heart and the way you talk. I think you came to us for a reason.

But if your debt is to be more than words you must pay it soon. For all our sakes.'

Gabble nodded. 'I'll try,' he said. And then, 'Please will you let Feather go? She should tell my clan about the Damplanders.'

'All right. I'll talk to Ar'bus. There's nothing to lose now.'

'Thank you.'

'So polite,' said Snip, but she did not smile. Then she left, following Ar'bus from the tunnel. Gabble stood alone, staring after their retreating forms and wondering what she thought he could do.

'Stupid, stupid,' Gabble muttered. 'Stupid rat.' He limped down the outside of the henburrow wall, keeping to the shadow and trying not to think about cats. The Damplanders were coming. Knowing this, any good ratling should be heading home, to tell his Akla. 'Stupid decision,' he told himself as his legs, stiff and sore, carried him ever further from the clanlands. 'Why aren't you going home? Heh?'

But he knew why. *I owe you a debt.* Words he had spoken. *I'll look after Ash, I promise.* Each word was nothing, a breath of wind, lost in the air. But they lodged and lived in rats' heads, making them think and act in new ways. He could feel these words in his own mind, binding him to this action with ties that the Hunter himself could not break. Everything was tangled, but through it all a single path shone, pale as moonlight. It led to Ash, to the Damplands. And so here he was, following Hope's scent. Soon it would cut across Notratlan and lead down the grassy margin to the Damplanders. The idea was terrifying, but still his feet kept moving.

A sound scuffled out from behind him. Gabble froze, shrinking into the shadows. A shape caught his eye, flashing in the moonshine as it broke out from a patch of shadow. He had the impression of massive amounts of fur whisking down the length of the wall, then an instant later Feather exploded into view, skidding to a panting stop beside him. Chest working, she glowered at him.

'You idiot!' she hissed. Then she shoved in beside Gabble in the shadows. For some moments neither rat spoke or moved, then Feather pattered back a few steps, to glare at him more effectively.

'What . . . in the name of . . . the Hunter . . . do you think you're doing?' she demanded. 'You nearly got eaten by a cat and now you're going for a walk to the Damplands? Are you stupid or something?'

Gabble bridled. 'Heh,' he said. 'It's not your business, I think.'

'Not my business?' Feather's voice was an outraged squeak. 'It was my business when I saved your life, you ungrateful flapfoot.'

The word 'flapfoot' brought a rush of anger. But then Gabble remembered the noise that had distracted the cat.

'That was you?'

'Of course it was me! Who did you think it was? The Hunter?'

'I didn't think,' said Gabble, flatly. 'There was a cat on top of me.'

Feather's brows lowered, dangerously.

'OK. Heh.' He raised a paw. 'You're right. I'm sorry. You saved me, and I'm being ungrateful. So thank you. But I still don't know why you were there.'

Feather looked a bit shifty. 'I followed you, of course.'

She had followed him. Of course. And why *wouldn't* the Bossrat's daughter follow a rat she barely knew all the way down to Notratlan? Unless he had told her to. Gabble put his head on one side.

'Ah, I see,' he said. Then, as reasonably as he could manage, he said, 'So maybe now it's best if you go back and tell your father where I am.'

Her reaction told him he had struck. She scowled and raised her paws, taking an aggressive step forwards.

'Don't pummel me. Heh,' said Gabble, backing away, 'I haven't done anything wrong.'

'Oh, really?' Her voice rose indignantly. 'Well, that's strange, isn't it? Because it looks to me like you're in Notratlan. After having been told never to come here again. And because of that I'm here too, and I don't like it.' Feather waved her paws around for emphasis as she spoke. Gabble had to duck to avoid being clouted. 'And if my father had told me to keep an eye on you he'd have been right, wouldn't he?' She gestured wildly at the stones around them. 'Because you're here!'

Oh, right. And this from someone who was sneaking around after other rats.

'Maybe your father's right,' said Gabble. 'And maybe he isn't. But you shouldn't be here.'

Feather's eyes blazed. 'And neither should you. You should be back at the clan.'

'I can't be.'

'What do you mean, "can't"? Of course you can.'

Gabble hesitated. If things went wrong, then somebody should warn the clan. But if they found out that Ash had gone to the Damplanders, then Ash was lost. He could never go home. Duty everywhere, pulling him one way and snapping back the other. Duty to his clan to be anywhere but here. Duty to Ash, to bring him home, keep him safe. Duty to Ar'bus to keep the Damplanders away. Gabble squeezed his eyes shut and breathed until his thoughts calmed.

'I'm going to the Damplands,' he said.

Feather's head whipped around in a blur of fur. 'You are not,' she said. 'I'm not going there.'

Gabble blinked. 'I never asked you to.'

'That doesn't matter.' A stony look glinted in Feather's eye. 'There's something else going on here. And you're going to tell me what it is.'

'I don't—'

Feather smacked him hard on the side of the head. Gabble jerked away. The movement tore at his half-healed muscles, making him wince.

'Don't hi—'

Another thump made his ears ring.

'Answer me!' Feather demanded. And then she hit him again, right on the ear. Gabble yelped and cradled his head. Feather raised her paw, threateningly, and something inside Gabble snapped. He rounded on her, paws raised and chest working.

'You really want to know?' he shouted. 'Do you? It's because of Ash. All right? It's because my stupid, thoughtless idiot of a brother has gone to the Damplanders and told them all about Notratlan.' He was angry at her, angry at Ash, angry at the world. 'Because they'll come here and take the eggs. And then maybe, with the Damplanders gorging themselves on Notratlan eggs, and crowding at our borders, our clan will have to fight. Maybe there'll be a war. And I don't know if any of that will happen, but I have to do my best to stop it.' He was shouting too loudly, he knew, but he couldn't stop himself. 'So maybe, if I can get there, and if they don't decide to just kill me, then

I can bring Ash home. Maybe I can make it so that everything will be all right again.' His voice broke off with a sob. Tears welled up and he shoved them angrily down. His vision blurred as he scowled at Feather. 'Now. Stop. Hitting. Me.'

Feather regarded him for some moments, then dropped to all fours. 'That's the most ridiculous thing I've ever heard,' she said. 'You don't even know if he's there.'

'Ash is there,' said Gabble. 'I met a Damplander who's seen him. So I'm going to find him.'

'But they'll kill you.'

'Maybe.'

Feather pattered closer, studying Gabble's face. She drew near enough for their whiskers to touch. The sensation made his mouth go oddly dry. When she was done she nodded once, as if satisfied and stepped back a pace.

'Right. Let's get going.'

Gabble blinked dazedly. 'What? Feather, I—'

'I thought,' she said, sweetly, 'that you wanted me to stop hitting you.'

'I do. But that's—'

'And you want to go to the Damplands.'

'Yes, but—'

'Then I'm coming too. So you'd better shut up and start walking, hadn't you?'

Gabble hesitated.

'*Hadn't you,*' Feather repeated. She raised a paw and studied it, meaningfully.

Gabble gave up. He had no reason to trust her, or to want her along. But he had no way of stopping her.

'Heh. Looks like it,' he said.

He started walking, staying close to the wall. Feather followed closely behind. Why she was here, what she wanted, and how this could ever work he had no idea. But somehow her presence made him feel better. He was going to the Damplands. But at least now he wasn't doing it alone.

Chapter nine

They moved quickly, dodging from cover to cover. The henburrow was long lost behind them. Their only guides now were Hope's scent and the ever-present Notratlan stone, glimpsed through the grass. Without these, Gabble could have believed that he and Feather were adrift, following a path from nowhere to nowhere. But as they moved, almost imperceptibly, the land changed around them. The air grew still, wet, and heavy. Dew formed and dripped, soaking their fur, and beading on their whiskers. The soil became spongy, and each footfall squeezed up water that glinted, briefly, before sinking away. And now at the field edge were scattered trees and shrubs that cast long shadows in the moonlight. Time slipped past, blurred by the tread of paws, the aching of legs and the routine of *scent, listen, dash*. But then, when it seemed to Gabble that there was no end to any of it, Notratlan simply stopped.

Gabble halted, up on his haunches, sniffing the air. The stone had ended, and now to every side lay open fields, broad plains of grass, dotted with oddly spiked rushes and bordered by ranks of trees. He jumped when Feather put a paw on his shoulder. He followed her gaze as she nodded silently up at the trees. There in the branches he saw a silhouette, hunched against the moon-hazed clouds. As he watched, it ruffled its feathers and settled back to motionlessness. Gabble swallowed. It was a bird of prey. Not an owl, thank the Mother, but some day-flier: a buzzard or kestrel. It was asleep, but its presence was a warning, to be under cover by daybreak. He scented carefully, and found Hope's trail. They followed it down through the grasses to where it joined a rat-run, laced with the Damplanders' scent. Gabble recoiled, cleaning his whiskers.

'This is it,' he whispered. 'The edge of the Damplands.'

Feather rolled her eyes. 'I can see that. I'm not thick, you know.'

Gabble sighed. She was determined to make life difficult.

'And stop that,' said Feather. 'I don't need you sighing at me.'

'I don't need you being a pest either,' Gabble hissed back. Feather's scowl deepened so quickly that Gabble took a hasty step back. 'Sorry,' he said, 'I'm just worried.'

'About what?'

'Everything. Heh. And I don't want you to get hurt.'

Feather's expression softened. 'But you'll be fine, I suppose?'

'I think the Damplanders won't hurt me.'

'Because of your brother?' said Feather.

Gabble nodded. 'They ran from him at that fight. I think they think he's the Taker or something. And we're brothers. We smell the same. So maybe I'll be OK.'

Feather considered him for long moments. And when she spoke again, her tone was almost gentle. 'Maybe,' she repeated. 'And then what? You'll find your brother, bring him out, and we head back to the clan?'

Gabble smiled. It was meant to look reassuring, but it probably wasn't. 'That's the plan,' he said. 'I have Ash's scent, my words, and a promise to keep. But if you come too, I think it won't work.'

Feather put her head on one side, as though she was going to argue.

A rat squeaked out sharply, 'Hey! Hey you!'

Gabble and Feather whirled toward the sound. But they saw nothing.

Another squeak. 'Who are you?'

Gabble spotted a nearby stand of grasses, the stems of which were trembling. He shot Feather a puzzled look. No attack had come, and the challenger sounded nervy and uncertain.

'How many?' Feather whispered.

'One, I think. Sounds scared.'

'Good. He should be.' She raised her chin. 'Who's that?' Feather demanded. 'What do you want?'

Gabble was impressed. She sounded like a rat with a perfect right to be there.

'It's me,' came the reply.

'Heh. Useful,' Gabble muttered. Feather made a shushing motion.

'Then stop skulking and come out here,' she called. 'Talk to us like a proper rat.'

Feather's tone said she expected to be obeyed. Gabble watched, amazed, as a scrawny male stepped reluctantly out into the open. The newcomer sidled out a few steps further, sniffing cautiously at the air. *The breeze is coming from behind him*, thought Gabble. *He can't smell us.*

'What you doing here?' the male asked between sniffs.

'We've been out,' said Gabble. 'And now we're back.'

The male absorbed this information, blinking at them. Not too quick in the head, apparently.

'Oh,' said the rat, eventually. ''Spose that's all right, then.'

Feather gave him a stern look. 'Well, of course it is,' she said. 'But well done for checking.' She nodded to Gabble. 'Come on.'

She set off at a brisk walk, leaving Gabble to scamper after her.

'Feather,' he hissed. 'Hang on, I have an idea.'

But he got no further. The breeze shifted, swirling scent to the guard rat, whose eyes widened.

'Hey!' he shouted. He came up on his haunches, vibrating with fear and excitement. 'I smell something. Stop there, I—'

And Feather was on him in an instant. There was a quick scuffle, and then Feather was settling down to groom her fur straight. Next to her the male lay dazed on the ground.

Gabble rushed to the male's side. 'You didn't have to do that,' he accused.

'I'm fine, thanks for asking,' said Feather, sarcastically. 'And I did too. He might have attacked or anything.'

'Attacked. Heh,' said Gabble, giving her a disapproving look. He pattered to where the male lay, head lolling woozily and forepaws paddling at the air. He was a young ratling and small for his age. His chest rose, imprinting the stark outline of ribs onto skin stretched taut beneath his thin fur. And, beneath the pungent Damplander's scent, Gabble smelled nervousness and eagerness to please. He sighed and sat back. This rat was not far off being a drudge. Feather joined Gabble, surveying the Damplander.

'Oh. Quite thin, isn't he?'

'Yes. Not a happy Damplander, I think.'

'So . . .' She gestured at the prone form. 'What do we do?'

Gabble gave her a rueful smile. 'Well, as I was trying to say, I have an idea.' It wasn't a great idea. In fact it was stupid, but, given that he was standing at the edge of the Damplands, about to hand himself to the Damplanders, everything was stupid anyway. 'This rat can take me to Ash.'

'He can *what*?'

The rat on the ground began to rouse himself, muzzily. 'No time to explain,' Gabble hissed. 'Find somewhere to hide. Stay safe and wait for me. I'll come back.'

'But—'

'Just do it! Please.'

The guard rat's head came up and his mouth opened as if trying to speak. His eyes rolled, blearily. For a nasty moment Feather looked as though she was going to argue. But then she nodded, and dashed for the nearest grasses, disappearing with a rustle.

And Gabble was alone with the Damplander.

The male raised his chin and focused on Gabble. He recoiled, raking at the ground in his desperation to get away. Gabble pattered after him.

'Hang on,' said Gabble, trying to sound harmless. 'Where are you going?'

'Don't hurt me,' the male squeaked, still scuttling for it.

Gabble feigned astonishment. 'I couldn't hurt a rat like you. You don't understand. I want to surrender.'

The male stopped dead and shot Gabble a look of mixed fear and suspicion. 'What?'

'I want to surrender. Heh.'

The male blinked. 'But—'

'I mean, I've never seen anything as brave as that. It was amazing,' said Gabble. 'That bird should have killed us both. I don't know how you fought it off.' Gabble gave a mock shudder. 'I thought it would take me. I owe you my life.'

Don't overdo it. He watched the male's face carefully. The male's confused expression began to fade.

'A—a bird?'

'Ooh, it was massive. Big beak,' said Gabble. 'It came for us. All I remember is it attacking, and then . . . I don't know. You were there, fighting it. And it flew away.' Gabble shook his head. 'Amazing.'

The male stared.

'Amazing. Heh,' said Gabble. 'So, I'll come with you,

like you said. Back to your clan.' Gabble was picking his words with great care. 'You saved me, so it's the only honourable thing to do.'

The male's brow began to furrow. Gabble thought fast. 'That's where you were going to take me, right? To your clan.'

The male glanced around. 'There was another rat,' he said. 'Here.'

Gabble did not glance at the tussock where Feather was hiding. 'She ran away,' he said. 'She was a coward.' He sincerely hoped that Feather hadn't heard that. The thumping wouldn't be fun. 'But you're not.'

The male's expression began to look something like pride. Or hope. He puffed out his spindly ribs. 'You'll come with me, right?'

'Right. Heh.'

'Then follow,' he said in an imperious tone. The male sprang away, heading for the main run. Gabble followed, not daring to glance back at Feather's tussock. He hoped she would be OK. He hoped she would wait for him to come back. He hoped he would come back.

The skinny rat rushed along, head down and paws pounding. He raced with his nose to the run, ears up, whiskers twitching, and eyes darting nervously here and there. He went so quickly that Gabble, his back half healed and his muscles stiff, could barely keep up. The run itself cut straight through the heart of the Damplands, and the Damplanders' disgusting scent was everywhere. It was pungent and alien, but even so Gabble could pick out details of the rats who lived here. He smelled the arrogant scent of the Bigrats—a few of those—and a muddle of many others, all lower. But through it all, different from the clan scent but still infusing every step of the run, was another, overpowering scent. It was repellent but familiar, nagging at Gabble's understanding.

The going underfoot grew wetter and the grasses gave way to rushes. And now the run skirted patches of black mud and thickened to a broad highway. And soon, round a bend, Gabble caught his first glimpse of their goal: a colossal embankment, half hidden by dense tangles of rank grasses, brambles, and nettles. Gabble's guide spotted it too. He began to lag, a fearful expression stealing across his face. Gabble turned to him with a curious look, but the male avoided his gaze, eyes down. Gabble felt a flash of pity. He had seen drudges at the Greenhedge but had never really thought about them. Seeing this rat he began to understand. He remembered the male's proud look at the thought of fighting off a bird. He had dreams like any other, but instead of the chance to follow them he had fear—fear of bigger rats. Gabble fell in alongside him.

'You beat me. Heh,' Gabble whispered. 'Head up, and be brave.'

But then a male, large and muscular, stepped into the run ahead of them, blocking the way. Gabble's companion stopped, quivering. And Gabble had no choice but to halt beside him. The big male ran an eye over the newcomers, and leered.

'Well, if it isn't a scrawnbag. Whatzit, Scrawnbag.'

Gabble's companion made a low sound, hunching down protectively, averting his gaze. 'W—whatzit, Na'dir. N—nice to see you.'

'Found a friend, have you?' Na'dir raised his voice, calling in a loud squeak. 'Come see: this scrawnbag's got a friend.'

Two more rats arrived with a scrabble of paws. One was piebald, and the other moved with a strange, cringing gait, as if half attacking, half shying away. But both were males, and both far bigger than Gabble. He raised his chin, meeting their gaze.

'Whatsat the scrawnbag got?' said the cringer.

'Not much, I reckons,' said the piebald rat.

'Me, I'd be leaving it where I found it.'

'With the other mice,' added Piebald, chortling at his own cleverness.

Scrawnbag shied back, simpering and cowering.

Gabble shifted uneasily. These rats' 'jokes' covered something hard. They were dangerous. He edged away, keeping them in view.

'Where's it going, I wonder?'

The laughter ceased. The three rats scurried forwards, fur raised. Gabble tensed, ready to run.

'Stay there,' Na'dir ordered. 'We need to know you.'

Gabble obeyed. Na'dir stepped in front of him. The other two ran around to his sides, preventing his escape. Gabble kept motionless. Beyond the rats, on the slopes of the embankment, Gabble could see others, darting across open ground or scratching at the earth. Some turned to watch the scene, or pattered closer, their faces alive with interest. Many more rats, though, lowered their heads and carried on, skirting the trouble and keeping to themselves. *Interesting*, thought Gabble.

A movement snagged Gabble's attention. He twisted aside as Na'dir's teeth snapped a fraction from his face. He scurried backwards—and ran into the rats behind him. Blows landed on his back and flank, and pain stabbed into his leg. Gabble wrenched around to face Cringer who was straightening with a nasty smile. Gabble glanced at the wound. It was a small bite. Enough to teach him a lesson.

'Got your attention, have we?' asked Cringer.

'Easy,' said Na'dir. 'Let's see what we have.'

Gabble stiffened as they sniffed at his flank.

'Greenhedge!' the first one spat. And before Gabble could move, he was pitched over and knocked to the ground. Teeth snapped from all sides. Gabble kicked out, keeping them from his body. A lucky blow landed with a squeak and an attacker staggered back, pawing at his nose. Gabble leapt up and danced beyond reach.

'Stay back,' he commanded. 'You don't know what you're doing.'

The males stopped, looking uncertain. Then Na'dir grinned.

'I know what I'm doing. I'm sending you to the Taker.'

Cringer leered at Gabble. 'Oh, bad for you, Greenhedge. Na'dir's a named rat.' He leaned forwards, lowering his voice to a mocking whisper. 'That means he's done it before.'

Gabble blinked. *Named rat*, he thought. *He's done it before*. Then the full significance of the words flooded into Gabble. A terrible feeling pulsed to his paws, to his tail: sorrow, anger, disbelief, sickness. And now he understood Ar'bus's hatred of the Damplanders. He could feel it too. Damplanders killed without thought or regret, that's what Ar'bus had said. But it was more than that. *There are no names. None but those we earn from the Taker.* The words echoed in Gabble's mind, heavy with new meaning.

'You kill,' said Gabble, his voice thick with outrage, 'for a name?'

'We honour the Taker,' said Na'dir, no longer smiling. 'We defeat our enemies.'

'I need myself a name,' said Piebald, snapping his teeth at Gabble. 'Might honour the Taker with his.'

'I won't no-say that,' said Na'dir, sizing Gabble. Piebald grinned and began to circle.

Thoughts poured into Gabble's mind; words to save him, to bring him to Ash.

'I have my own honour,' said Gabble. 'It takes me to Rai'thir.'

Rai'thir. That was a name that Hope had used back in the henburrow. She had spoken of him as though he was a rat to respect. It was a desperate attempt, but Piebald stopped dead.

'The Akla?' he said.

Oh, thank the Mother.

'Yes, I must see him,' said Gabble. And as he spoke his gaze was searching the surrounding lands, looking for Scrawnbag. He spotted him in a stand of rushes, just his nose poking out. Gabble nodded at the rushes. 'He's taking me there. That rat there. He defeated me.'

Na'dir's eyes widened. 'What? That *scrawnbag?*'

Gabble nodded. 'That's right.'

Na'dir dived for the rushes and reappeared, dragging

out the squeaking Scrawnbag. He thrust the skinny rat into the middle of the circle. Scrawnbag faced the three huge rats, a terrified expression on his face.

Na'dir gestured at Gabble. 'Is he saying truth? You defeated him?'

Scrawnbag wheeled around, giving Gabble a desperate look. Gabble forced a reassuring smile, and placed a paw on Scrawnbag's shoulder. 'It's OK,' he murmured. 'Tell them. Remember the bird.'

Scrawnbag straightened slightly. 'Yes,' he said, with desperate defiance. 'I did.'

And now the three rats were looking more uncertain.

'He knows something you don't,' said Gabble, talking smoothly, keeping them unsure. 'I may be from the Greenhedge, but so is your white rat.' The others tensed at the mention of Ash. Good. 'And if you had scented carefully you'd have smelled the white rat's mark on me. Because I'm his brother.'

Piebald and Cringer began to back away. Scrawnbag's mouth dropped open. Only Na'dir stayed where he was, nose twitching as he drew down Gabble's scents. Then his eyes narrowed, and a nasty smile spread across his face.

'So,' he said, 'brother, is it? And going to Rai'thir?'

And that was too much for Scrawnbag. At Rai'thir's name he uttered a low squeak and fled, paws flying, back down the run. Gabble gazed after him.

'I was. Heh. But I might just go and see my brother instead.'

'I reckon,' said Na'dir, squaring up, 'that I can take you to the Akla.'

At his gesture the other rats surrounded Gabble.

'Heh,' Gabble muttered. 'I thought you might say that.'

Gabble was shoved and jostled, Na'dir ahead, and the others behind, to the foot of the embankment. It loomed above them, a massive and imposing heap of earth, nettles and rat runs. He tried to stay calm, to ignore the blood that rushed in him, the feeling that said, *You are going to the Damplanders' burrow. Run.* Passing rats stared, alerted by his foreign smell, but they dropped their gazes at aggressive squeaks from Na'dir. They stepped obediently aside as Na'dir passed, but Gabble could feel their gazes, resentfully lingering.

They urged Gabble up a short, well-trodden slope up to a low valley, almost a notch in the embankment wall. Gabble laboured up the incline, ignoring the teeth that nipped at him, until he crested the hill and found himself on a flat area, looking out across a huge expanse of water. The embankment stretched away, forming an almost complete ring around the outside of a lake. It met the water in a glistening flat of mud and water plants. Illuminated in the moonglow the lake sparkled with black and silver ripples. And beyond it a hint of water ran like a ribbon through the landscape. Gabble had never seen anything like it. Everything was breath-catchingly beautiful, even here, even now. He stared until a solid nip on his flank brought his attention back.

'Follow me, Greenhedge,' Na'dir ordered, and set off uphill, making for a nearby burrow. The smell emanating from inside made Gabble gag, but with the rats behind he had no choice but to pick his way up the refuse-laden slope, and then, paws trembling, to step inside. The interior was terrible. He told himself that it was just a smell, that it was just different, that's all. But he knew that was a lie. The stench pounded his senses, pouring its wrongness into him. And now, immersed in the heart of it, Gabble knew what it was made of: it was fear, and it was everywhere. This was not panic, fresh fear, or a response to an immediate threat, but far, far worse. It was fear that was old and hardened until it had become normal, a part of life. Generations of rats had woven their dread into every turn and corner of the burrow until it seemed to rise from the earth itself. The whole colony was quiet, subdued—no bustle and chatter here, but muted and sporadic scratchings and unseen scurrying, quick through dark tunnels. So this was where Hope had been born, and where Ash must have come. It filled Gabble with creeping horror.

'Nice burrow' he said, trying to talk away his unease. 'Heh. I like the quiet.' His attempt drew no response from the Damplanders behind.

'Keep moving,' said Na'dir, curtly, and led off.

'Right you are.'

They followed a tunnel that ran in a flat curve, tracking the pond's edge. Then it dipped down through the ground, towards the heart of the embankment. The unseen scrabbling was more urgent here, the pattering of paws faster. It gave Gabble a vision of rats running from something that lurked in the ground beneath him. But that was stupid. The burrow depths should be a rat's refuge, the place of greatest safety. Gabble glanced back. Na'dir's friends had kept pace, still blocking any retreat. This far down any light was gone, but he sensed their presence from their breathing and the sound of their paws. Gabble's whiskers brushed the soil, stirring scents that wormed into his nostrils, bitter and unwelcome. He would have given anything to groom them from his nose, then to turn and run. But he carried on down, deeper into the ground, putting more turns and more Damplanders between him and escape.

He hesitated at a junction, unsure of which turn Na'dir had taken.

'Move. That way.' Paws urged him forwards and teeth nipped at his leg.

'Ouch, all right,' said Gabble, scampering forwards. 'Your hospitality needs work, I think.'

After that they moved in silence until, abruptly, the tunnel broadened. To each side the walls fell away and the footsteps behind ceased. Gabble heard a faint shuffling of the paws, and the sound of breath, but Piebald and Cringer had stopped. Deprived of guides and features, Gabble too stopped, fighting disorientation. The chamber was close and airless, and the burrow smell was pungent. A muted conversation echoed from somewhere ahead, Na'dir's voice wheedling and that of another rat in low tones. Gabble strained to listen but could hear no words. But he knew without question, from Na'dir's respectful tone, and the anxious breathing of the rats behind him, that the other rat was Rai'thir, the Damplanders' Akla. The murmuring ended and Na'dir approached, breathless in the dark.

'The Akla will speak with you,' said Na'dir. His voice sounded shaky, as though he were relieved to be away from the Akla's burrow. He pushed past Gabble, and ran a short way down the tunnel behind. Now all three rats were back there, barring the way, and Gabble was left with no option. His paws clenched, but he raised his chin and called out into the darkness.

'I have come to see my brother,' said Gabble. His nails dug into the ground. 'My thanks for allowing me into your burrow.'

Something about the darkness gave an air of consideration. And then a voice, close by and powerful, spoke.

'Indeed you have come to us, just as I foretold. You may enter.'

The Akla's tone was smooth and deep. It reminded Gabble of the moonlit lake. But this lake-water was black, and something bubbled beneath its surface. Some vast form ran around Gabble and circled in the dark, blocking his retreat. Whiskers brushed against his fur.

'Enter,' the voice insisted, now from behind.

And Gabble, skin crawling, moved up the tunnel into the Akla's reeking chambers.

chapter ten

'This night is exceptional.' Rai'thir's smooth voice flowed out from the entrance. The darkness here was absolute, but Gabble sensed that these chambers were vast, buried deep and away from the other rats. 'This night the Shining One's brother stands in my burrow.'

The Shining One. Gabble flinched, then schooled himself to stillness. 'Yes. I'm Ash's brother,' he said.

'Ash. Ah, a Greenhedge pupname.' Rai'thir spoke without inflection, betraying nothing. Each word was polished, as though carefully selected before being spoken. His tone was mild, but his scent thickened the air, cloying and powerful. It was the odour of a rat who was the master of his world. 'We have no use for those, here.'

Gabble swallowed. In Rai'thir's presence he found it

hard to think, or speak. 'Y—you have only true names?'

'True names. Quite,' said Rai'thir. 'Why did you come here?'

The question rapped out, abrupt. And Gabble heard, distinct in the unnatural silence, the sound of Rai'thir's paws, treading their stealthy way closer. The Akla's smell intensified, clagging in Gabble's nostrils, bearing down into his mind and muddying his thoughts. Gabble stood, petrified, as Rai'thir crept to within striking distance. Rai'thir's breath ruffled Gabble's fur. Gabble battled the urge to hit out and dash away, to sprint down the tunnels for open spaces and clean air. To do any of that would mean death.

'Answer me, ratling, and do not lie,' Rai'thir whispered in Gabble's ear. 'I can smell lies. It's a gift.'

I can smell lies. The words repeated in Gabble's mind. *It's a gift.* But Gabble too had a gift. He had words that danced, that changed the thoughts in other rats' heads. And now, despite the hammering of his blood and the trembling of his whiskers, Gabble found the ghost of a smile on his lips. He was certain that this rat would kill him in an instant, and any lie he spoke would turn his words against him. But what if he could answer without a lie? *A dance like the Trickster's*, Gabble thought. *A dance with words.* He closed his eyes.

'Simple. Heh. I came for my brother. I promised I would. And it seemed like a nice night.'

A pause. Then sniffing, sniffing. Whiskers too close, brushing Gabble's flank, intruding on his past and seeking his secrets. A silence.

'You are the brother of the Shining One, of that you spoke truly. You are from his clan. But I smell the marks of another rat, not Greenhedge, not Chosen. You will explain.'

'The mark is from Notratlan.' No point in denying it. If Hope was right then Ash had told Rai'thir all about Ar'bus and the henburrow. 'I went there for my brother. I fought with some rats there.'

More scenting sent chills of revulsion cascading to Gabble's paws. But he did not move.

'Notratlan. Yes, that is truth.' Rai'thir withdrew a pace. 'Many of our Chosen have gone to the Taker seeking Notratlan. How did you live when they did not?'

'Chosen?' asked Gabble.

'My clan. The Taker's Chosen. Now answer: why did you live?'

'Notratlan is guarded by a cat,' said Gabble. 'It was that that killed your Chosen. I fought it and drove it away. And then I came here.'

Again whiskers brushed Gabble's flank, sniffing, sniffing for his secrets. Gabble tensed, but each word he had spoken had been the truth. And each scent Gabble carried would prove it.

'So the Shining One's brother comes to us from Notratlan.' And now Rai'thir's tone was musing. 'And he has fought a cat.'

'Yes,' said Gabble. 'And now, I'd like to see Ash. I've come a long way. Heh.'

This was the speech of another rat, a stronger and more confident rat. Part of Gabble shrank in fear, but part of him was that rat, exalting in the effect of his words.

'You might speak with the Shining One,' said Rai'thir, chill amusement in his voice. 'But were I to allow it, what then?'

A warning rang in Gabble's mind. This question held a trap. He could feel the shape of it, hanging in the air. It was an invitation to give the wrong response. And if he did then Gabble's life would be snapped out. He closed his eyes. What were the right words? What would a Damplander wish to hear?

'Then I will have done what I promised.'

'You will return to your clan?'

'My clan?' Gabble chuckled, and the sound had a bitter edge. 'When I left my clan I defied my Akla. Heh. He won't welcome me back.' Gabble let the words flow. They spun from his tongue, twisting the truth, and making it dance. 'I came here, knowing that any of you might end my life. I did it for Ash. I want to see him and then I will go to the Taker.'

Yes, I'll go to the Taker, Gabble thought, *but hopefully after a long life and far, far from here.*

Silence, filled only with the rush of Gabble's blood, thrumming in his body. Everything he had said had been both true and a lie. Which had Rai'thir heard?

'And are you afraid?' The question slipped into the air, mild as a breeze. But somehow this question too was a test. Gabble frowned in the dark.

'Rats who are afraid meet the Taker every night,' he answered, carefully. 'I will meet him only once. I'll give him my name and then we'll see.'

But the moment the words were loose Gabble knew he had made a mistake.

'You are not like the Chosen,' said Rai'thir with a hiss. 'You have no name.'

And Rai'thir was on him, grasping and shaking him. Gabble was ripped from the ground and hurled against the burrow wall. The collision knocked the air from him, and he gasped there, flooding with fear. He struggled for breath, trying to roll to his feet, to defend himself. But he knew it was hopeless. The memory of Rai'thir's touch filled him with horror. The rat's polished words were a mask, hiding colossal, brutish strength. The huge rat prowled closer, poised to end Gabble's life.

'I have a name, one that I earned from the Taker,' Gabble gasped out, repeating in his desperation the words that Hope had used.

Rai'thir hesitated. 'What do you mean?' he snarled.

It was a reprieve, just for a moment. Gabble clambered to his feet, shaking.

'I met one of your clan. I took her name from her.'

'If you lie . . .' Rai'thir hissed. And Gabble was knocked back once more by Rai'thir's strength. But this time the Akla grabbed him, wrenching his body this way and that as his nose and whiskers interrogated Gabble's fur. And all the while Rai'thir's thick odour swirled around Gabble, forcing itself onto his coat and into his mind.

'I speak . . . the truth,' Gabble managed. *Just not the truth as you see it. I took Hope's name with my words. It was not a name that any of your Chosen would recognize, but it was hers. And then I returned it to her, with her life.*

At last Rai'thir released him, and stepped away. 'Yes,' he said. 'I smell her on you. I smell her defeat. And I hear truth in your words,' said Rai'thir. And now his voice was smooth again. But, Gabble realized, with a new note. He sounded almost eager. 'So you are named. You are a true rat. You live like the Chosen.'

Only an effort of will prevented Gabble collapsing to the floor. 'I live as I live,' he stammered. 'I don't know about your Chosen.'

'We are the Taker's Chosen,' said Rai'thir softly. 'He is the rat that all of us must meet.' His voice was now little more than a whisper, but filled the spaces of the burrow. It had a strange quality, rich and enticing. 'It's in the oldest tale. The Mother feared to give the Taker her heart, for she knew him to be the strongest of the three brothers. She feared that with a heart he would become more powerful than she. So she imprisoned him in the Land of Bones.' Rai'thir's words wove in the air, inviting Gabble to believe. 'Each rat carries a piece of the Mother's heart, and the Taker draws it to him. One day he will have enough of the heart to break free, and then he shall rule.'

Gabble found himself nodding, almost understanding Rai'thir's twisted vision of the world. Rai'thir's voice was whispering, coaxing. 'Oh, that day will be glorious. The end of death, when all rats shall live in the world beyond. But until then we must honour the Taker. We send rats to him, each carrying their fragment of heart. And for this service he grants our names, plucked from the heart of the rat we have slain. I am the Chosen's Akla. I give my rats their names from the Taker. And when they die he will greet each one as a friend, and guide them to the world beyond.'

'And the rats you kill?' asked Gabble. 'What happens to them?'

'Ah.' Rai'thir sidled nearer. 'If they fight like true rats then they die trying to send the Taker their enemy's heart. They honour him and they too will go to the world beyond.' The words coiled in Gabble's mind, forming shapes both repellent and attractive. 'Only drudges need to fear. Only the rats too cowardly to fight will go nameless and their bones will fall to the ground in the Taker's domain. The rest of us are Chosen, and we fear nothing. We are free. We fight and we win, or we die in the fight. Either way we honour the Taker, and we will live in the world beyond.'

Life beyond death, the Taker greeting him as a friend. Gabble turned the ideas in his mind. He could feel his desire for them. After everything he had done to meet his promises, how scared he had been and all he had lost, to think that he could have lived without fear, or duty. What did it matter if he failed Ash or the Mothers? All he needed to do was fight. But something about the thought was hollow. Gabble remembered the looks the other rats had given Na'dir. He remembered the stench of fear, and the desperation that infused the Damplanders' burrow. Why, if Rai'thir's words were true, would those rats smell like that?

And Gabble realized, with a shock of revulsion, that Rai'thir had not given the Damplanders freedom. No, he had taken everything from them. They had no pupname to shape them, no true name from their Mothers that they could live by. Only to those willing to kill for him would Rai'thir grant a name. The rest would die nameless, without a hope of passing to the world beyond. No wonder they looked at the Bigrats like that. Names were a part of who you were, a rat's greatest gift, given by those who loved them. A name, Ar'bus had said, was a sign that you lived a true life, and had kept your heart pure for the Taker. How could any rat live as they did, without a name, or the hope of one—unless they killed.

Gabble recalled his promise to the Mothers, and his friend, Feather, who was waiting for him. He remembered Ar'bus, Snip, and Shrill, and how they had helped him after the cat. He remembered the war that could destroy his clan. His name was Fo'dur, the Shining One. And to live it well meant he must keep his promises. And in the face of these things Rai'thir's words became nothing but air.

'I see,' he said. 'I understand. You have shown me the path of the Chosen. So I will live and be glad of my name. Heh. And Ash? Is he Chosen too?'

'The Taker sent him to us as a sign,' said Rai'thir. 'We shall follow him from this burrow, and he will lead my clan to their names. Your brother is, after all, called the Shining One.'

Gabble did not dare move. But he thought, *that name was never his. Fo'dur is my name. And you are following a lie.*

'The Shining One,' he said. 'I always knew Ash was special. Can I see him?'

'Of course. You should go to your brother,' said Rai'thir, as if that had always been his intention.

'Thank you,' said Gabble. 'I am glad that we spoke.'

Rai'thir scented the air one last time and made a small sound, almost of satisfaction. 'Leave,' he said. 'And send me Na'dir.'

He stepped aside, leaving access to the world beyond his chambers. Gabble walked towards the tunnel, trying not to stumble on his shaking legs.

The three rats outside shrank away at Gabble's approach. *Now they're afraid of me*, thought Gabble. *They expected me to die in there. And I must reek of Rai'thir's scent, like one of his Chosen.* The thought sickened him, but he did not touch his fur. Instead he lifted his head.

'Na'dir,' he said. 'You're here. I can smell you.'

'I'm here.'

'Your Akla wants you.'

Rats shifted uncertainly in the darkness.

'Now. Heh.'

Na'dir disappeared into Rai'thir's burrow. Gabble heard his stammering and Rai'thir's powerful voice. Then Na'dir rejoined them with a quick scurry.

'I'll take you to the Shining One,' he said. His bragging tone was gone, replaced almost with respect. 'Follow.'

This time there were no commands, and no nipping teeth. The other rats fell away, running gratefully off to their own business. And Na'dir led Gabble, unspeaking, through the tunnels, making for higher ground. Gabble for his part did not want to talk. Ash was waiting for him, somewhere in this horrible burrow. But how would it be when they met? And what would he do then?

The tunnel curved up to a junction, somewhere in the centre of the embankment. There Na'dir took another broad path that led away along the embankment's length, staying away from the outside walls. The Damplanders were keeping Ash right in the heart of their clan. But here at least some light penetrated, casting a murky glow onto the soil.

'In there,' said Na'dir, stopping in front of a gloomy entrance. 'The Shining One is inside. You can nest there, if you want.'

'My brother's chambers,' said Gabble. 'Good. Now you may go.'

Na'dir showed his teeth, but lowered his head. 'As you say,' he said. And then he left down the tunnels.

Gabble watched him go, and breathed a sigh. Then he turned to face the burrow entrance, whiskers twitching. At first he could smell nothing but Damplanders, but then he caught a wisp, a trace of a scent, familiar from puphood. The smell tightened his throat, making his eyes sting with tears. But this was the Damplands, and no place for crying. Gabble swallowed hard, and walked down towards the chambers, sinking once again into darkness. He followed his nose and whiskers until he came to an occupied chamber. He paused at the entrance until he was certain that the smell of his brother rose from within. Then he stepped into the room.

He heard a soft rustle of fur on grasses as something, huddled against the far wall, shifted its position. And Gabble heard a crackling noise, and a stifled cough. Ash was here. *Oh, thank the Mother.* His brother was here, and alive.

'Whatzit, Ash,' Gabble murmured.

More rustles, then, 'I know this scent.' Ash's voice, muzzy from sleep.

'You should,' said Gabble. 'You've known it long enough.'

Ash pulled himself from his bedding and coughed. 'Ah, Gabbley,' he said. 'Now that's funny. Whatzit, Gabble.'

Gabble ran to him, searching Ash's fur with whiskers and paws, seeking his brother amidst the scents that smothered him. Ash stood stiffly for a moment, and then he clutched for Gabble's fur. They clung together for some moments before Ash pulled away.

'You smell weird,' said Ash.

'*I* smell weird? You smell awful.' Rai'thir had smeared his scent all over Ash in thick smudges, as though he wanted to own him. 'You smell like a Damplander.'

'Do I? Ah. Well, I should.'

'No you shouldn't. And you said it's funny. What's funny?'

'You. You always follow me, don't you?'

'That's true. Heh. I haven't learned.'

'No,' said Ash, abruptly serious. 'You haven't. You shouldn't be here.'

'Right. And neither should you. So how do we get out?'

'We? Gabble, I'm not leaving. This is where I belong. Rai'thir explained it to me.' Ash spoke quickly, urgently. 'Rai'thir told me and it made sense. Now I can see what I am.'

Gabble snorted. 'So can I. You're an idiot.' He shook his head. 'What in the name of the Mother is wrong with you?'

'Nothing's wrong with me, Gabbley. I'm the same as I always was.' And for a moment Gabble could almost have believed that. But then a coughing fit gripped Ash. Gabble heard movements, angry in the dark as Ash fought it, and dragged down a ragged breath. 'Don't . . . look at me like that,' he rasped. 'I can feel you watching me. I don't need your pity. You think . . . this is wrong. Well, it isn't.'

His voice was savage. 'This, this is me. This is my body bearing the Taker's mark. I'm not afraid to be who I am.'

'That's not what you said before. You said your future had been taken.'

'Before. Hah! *Before* I hadn't met Rai'thir. Before I didn't know.' Ash was almost shouting. 'I am the Shining One. I belong to the Taker. He marked me and brought me here, to the Chosen. So many of them are nameless, Gabble. I can give them what they need. I can name them. I can help them.'

'You mean take them to Notratlan?'

Ash laughed, and the sound rang hollow in Gabble's ears. 'Of course! Why else did the Taker guide me there? Notratlan and eggs, and names for the Chosen.'

Gabble almost could not breathe. 'Ash,' he said quietly, 'rats live in Notratlan. Good rats. What will your Chosen do to them to get their names?'

'Maybe they'll send them to the Taker,' said Ash. 'But if they fight, then the Taker will guide them to the world beyond.'

The words sent a chill through Gabble. 'You're sure of that, are you? What if they just fight and die? Heh?'

'You still don't understand, do you?' Ash rasped. 'I *saw* him. He's real. He gave me my name. I'm the Shining One. My fur shines like the Taker's moon. I will use my brightness as a symbol to lead the Chosen to him.' Ash's voice was full of cold pride. 'I am the Shining One.'

'No, Ash, you're not,' said Gabble. 'I came here to tell you that. Fo'dur is my name, not yours. When you were ill I told you my name to make us brothers, to bind us together. You heard it, and, oh, I don't know, you dreamt of the Taker or something.' Gabble came forwards, and put his paws on Ash's shoulders. 'Ash, you never heard your true name. You heard mine.' Ash stayed silent, so Gabble poured words into the space between them, trying to bring his brother back. 'But it doesn't matter. None of it does. My name is big enough for us to share. Come back with me. Please. Then we'll be true brothers, sharing our name.'

But Ash laughed at him from the darkness. 'Oh, Gabble, I'm sorry.'

'Sorry? What for?'

'You. I'm sorry for you. You always thought you were here to protect me, didn't you?' Gabble said nothing. 'Didn't you?' Ash shouted, abruptly wrenching Gabble's paws away and rounding on his brother. 'But you weren't protecting me; you were stopping me from being me. And now I've finally become what you could never be, you've come here to steal my name.' Ash came forwards, breath hissing. 'Well, Rai'thir told me this would happen. Jealousy, that's what he said.

Others would be jealous that I saw the Taker, that he chose me. You're jealous that I'm special.'

'Nobody chose you,' said Gabble. 'You got ill and you took my name. You won't hear the truth.'

'And you won't see it,' Ash snapped. 'I have white fur. I weep as the Taker wept. I cry red tears.'

'It was the Mother who wept red tears, not the Taker,' Gabble replied, softly. 'She cried for his loneliness.'

'No,' Ash hissed. 'I saw him. He whispered my name to me in words that burned. I am the Shining One, and I will do what he asks.'

'And did the Taker tell you to lead this clan to Notratlan? Or was that Rai'thir's idea?' Gabble demanded. He sensed Ash's hesitation. 'Because Ar'bus will fight you with his life, and still the Damplanders will win. And then your *Chosen* will go on to Greenhedge. Our Mothers, Ash. Our clan. The Damplanders will destroy our home to get their names. Is that what you want?'

'Can't you see it's not like that?' Ash cried. 'They'll honour the Taker and go to the world beyond. Does that sound so bad?'

'Yes,' said Gabble. 'It sounds terrible. Ash, if you want my name then fine, we share it. But there's more than one way to shine.' He let go a breath and opened his paws. 'Look at me. I'm not big, and I'm no different to any other rat. I'm scared out of my mind but I came here anyway. I came after you, because in all the world there's nobody I love more than you. Isn't that also what it means to be called the Shining One? Being afraid, but doing what's right?' His eyes searched the darkness, seeking any sign that Ash was listening, that his mind could be changed. 'You've lost a lot, I can see that, but you don't have to lose yourself as well. Come away with me. We have a name. It's Fo'dur. And it's big enough to share. We don't need anything else.'

Ash's breath bubbled in the black of the burrow. He was silent for the longest time, then said, 'No. The Taker marked me. I am his, like I always was. I'll do what he wants.'

'The Taker marks all of us,' Gabble replied, sadly. 'Every rat will meet him, but that doesn't make us his. I have my own path to follow.' Gabble tapped his chest. 'It's in here, with my name and my heart. I will give them to him when I die, but not before.' Gabble turned to go. 'I came here for my brother, but I found the Shining One. I wish I had found Ash instead.'

Then he walked from the chamber. And he sensed, as he left, Ash's unseeing eyes, gazing balefully out from the darkness.

Gabble willed his body on down the tunnel. He was exhausted, filled with grief, and desperate in his need to rest, to heal. But he had done what he came for, and now everything in him urged him out, out of these fear-soaked tunnels and away from Rai'thir and the rat his brother had become. And somewhere in the Damplands, if the Hunter had protected her, Feather would be waiting. He needed her strength and her help. In the end, it seemed, his words had not been enough.

He wound his way out from the burrow interior and the tunnel walls lightened around him, black to grey to dingy brown. The air freshened, ushering scents from the outside. Gabble drank them in, letting them pull him onward. Finally he rounded a bend, and daylight, whitish and brutal, flooded over him. It splashed across his face, red through his screwed-tight eyes. Daylight. Heh. *Only fools and drudges go out in the day*. That's what the Mothers had taught him. *But the Trickster favours the foolish*. Daylight meant that the Damplanders would be in their chambers. Daylight gave Gabble a chance.

He ran quickly and stealthily, nosing his way to the air. Then he stopped dead. The tunnel was blocked by a hulking form, blotted black by the dazzling sun beyond. Gabble crouched, tail twitching. It was a rat, and asleep, and there was no way past without waking it. Gabble cursed silently, and backed away. He retraced his steps to the nearest junction, selected a different turn, and headed once more for the outside. But at this entrance too, a rat blocked his path. This one was intent on grooming, though, and Gabble crept away, unseen. He ran back to Ash's chambers, then followed the tunnel past, taking a flat path that split then dipped down to the base of embankment. Again the tunnel lightened, and he slowed, slinking paw over paw and making as little noise as he could. *He must get out. He must.*

Once more the air became fresh, but even as hope filled him, Gabble breasted a curve to find a rat in the entrance. This time the guard was smaller, and its back was to him, nose to the incoming breeze. Gabble wanted to beat the ground in frustration. These rats had surely not all just decided to sleep in the tunnels. Gabble might have convinced Rai'thir for now, but the Damplander's Akla wasn't stupid. Gabble had been effectively imprisoned. He sat back, thinking. He could take another route, but even if the Damplanders had left a path unguarded, it would take time to find, and every moment he was out in the burrow was a risk, that he would be detected and questioned. But perhaps there was another way.

He crept forwards, scenting carefully. The morning breeze carried the guard's scent up to him. A female, and one, he realized, whose scent was familiar. He suppressed a smile. The Trickster really did favour the foolish. He moved stealthily up to within a pace of her.

'Whatzit,' he whispered.

The female jumped, banging her head on the tunnel roof. She spun, ready to shout or fight. Her eyes widened.

'What are *you* doing here?'

'Hello, Hope,' said Gabble.

'Don't ever say that word,' she hissed, glancing around. 'I told you, I have no name. Now answer me. What are you doing?'

'Trying to stay alive. Heh,' said Gabble. 'And it's not very easy.'

Hope blinked at him, then pressed her lips together. 'So you're the one,' she said. 'We're not supposed to let you out.'

'That's a problem, then,' said Gabble. 'They told you to block the tunnels, did they?'

Hope nodded. 'Yes, Na'dir did.' Hope's lip curled as she spoke the name.

Gabble nodded. Of course he had. On Rai'thir's orders. 'Then I need you to let me go.'

Hope began to shake her head, and lifted a paw, uncertainly.

'Please,' said Gabble. 'My brother, the white rat: he's going to lead you to Notratlan.'

Hope's head came up. And, for the first time since Gabble had met her, her eyes were bright. 'But that's good, isn't it? He'll take us to where we can earn our names. That's what Rai'thir says.'

Gabble dropped his gaze. 'Maybe,' he said. 'Maybe you'll earn a name, and maybe you'll be a Bigrat, who gets the best food. But what happens when there aren't enough names to go around, and when there aren't enough rats to fight? What happens when most of your clan are still nameless? Heh? Will you start killing my clan, the Greenhedge, thinking that that's what the Taker wants, but mostly for a name?' Hope was staring at Gabble as though she could not understand what he was saying. 'Is that how it will be?' he demanded. 'Will your clan just fight and raid and spread until everyone is *Chosen* and there's no one left to kill?'

Gabble realized he was nearly sobbing. He swallowed, and unclenched his paws. 'I'm sorry,' he said. 'It's not your fault. But I have to go. I have to do something about this.'

'I can't,' said Hope. 'I can't let you out.'

'Yes you can.' Gabble offered her a tremulous smile. 'It's easy. You just step aside.'

'Why should I?'

'Ah. Heh. Because I know that despite what you say, you already have a name. I know what your Mother wished for you. And I know that a name, even a pupname, should be lived.'

Hope stared at Gabble for so long than he wondered if she would ever move or speak again. Then, tentatively she reached out a paw, and touched his fur. She withdrew it quickly, and looked away.

'Go, then,' she said. 'I'll give you as much time as I can.'

Gabble eased past Hope and stood in the burrow entrance. He glanced back at her. Her gaze was still fixed on the ground, and she would not look at him.

'Thank you,' he said.

And then he was away down the tunnel and sprinting for daylight.

Chapter eleven

The low sun dazzled from every surface. Soon it would chase the shadows into the earth and expose the world to the eyes of the predators. Half blinded by light and weak with fatigue, Gabble would be easy prey. He staggered on, stumbling off the last of the burrow slopes. He splashed through streams and rivulets, forging down the main run with gritted determination to put distance between him and the Damplanders' burrow.

Soon his muscles were burning, and the breath was scant in his chest. He came to a junction and stopped, gratefully drawing down cool air as he scented for the path ahead. He glanced back at the bank of burrows, rising up above the rushes, and shook his head. It could have been a rat's paradise, a deep, warm bank surrounded by birds, bramble fruit, seeds, and frogs. But deep in its heart it was poisoned. Its fear stretched out down these runs, flowing into the lands beyond. And in there was Ash, who needed him now more than ever. All Gabble's words had not shaken the grip that Rai'thir held on his brother's mind. If Gabble were the Trickster from the stories he would have used his wits to dance them both to freedom. But such dances, it seemed, were not for real rats.

He pulled his gaze back to the road ahead, but not before he caught a movement in the plants at the base of the mound. He heard voices call out, and saw nettles bowing, thrust aside by something that followed swiftly down the route he had taken. Gabble began to back away, scampering, then turning and sprinting, racing for the edge of the Damplands. And, in response, the sounds from behind grew louder. Rats were coming for him.

No time to think now, just to move. His whiskers and nose tracked the path, his paws pelted, and his body swayed and weaved between tussocks. He must get to Feather, and trust that she had waited. Head down and panting, he heard his pursuers draw closer. Terror gripped him, but he shoved it away, forcing his body onward, and making it use the last of its strength. Gabble's paws threw up spray and ripped at wet earth. But for all his efforts, he knew he was weak. Hungry and thirsty, his back only half healed, and his muscles raw, the Damplanders would catch him. They would fight him, and win.

'No!' The sound growled out, savage from Gabble's throat. Feather was there up ahead, someone to run to, something to push for. She would be waiting. *Please, she had to be waiting.* He held the thought of her, bright in his mind, as the world wheeled around him, as his senses drowned in the agony of limbs pushed to their limits, and lungs that could not meet his need for air. Plants whipped his face. Grasses crowded the way and the ground grew drier. And some distant part of Gabble saw that the run had dwindled to a slender track, that he was close to the edge of the Damplands. Joy surged in him. Here was the place where he had met Scrawnbag, where Feather should be. He stumbled to a stop in the centre of a grassy hollow, gasping for air. Then he wrenched himself around to face his pursuers.

'Feather!' His breath whooped as he refilled his lungs. Feather, help! Please, I need help!'

No response.

'Feather!'

Why didn't she answer? Had she left? Was she hiding? Where was she?

And then a shriek rang out from the sky. Gabble's head snapped up and he raked the shining expanse for the source of the sound. There, all but lost against the brightness, a shape hovered. Spread feathers, a bent head with a beak designed for ripping, and wings that fluttered, locking the bird in the air. It was a kestrel. And he had not seen it.

Gabble went utterly still, his only movement a trembling in his jaw and chest. He had fled from the Damplanders into a kestrel's hunting grounds. And now he was far from cover, exposed in the flat centre of a ring of grass tussocks. He stared up at its hovering form, not daring even to blink. He could not escape. The wings would fold, and the kestrel would stoop. It would take him.

Grasses rustled as a rat eased out of the clearing's edge. Gabble, eyes locked on the predator above, did not even glance at it. But he knew who it was: Na'dir's scent curled in the air. Only Na'dir's, though. He must have outrun the others.

'Whatzit, Hunter,' Na'dir panted. 'You tried it . . . didn't you?'

And, as if Na'dir's words had given him permission to move, Gabble began to move, inching almost imperceptibly away to the edge of the clearing.

'Na'dir,' he whispered, 'you need to listen to me.'

Na'dir laughed nastily. 'I've heard enough words from you.' He stepped fully out from his cover. 'What you've done is you've lied to me. And you won't do that more than once.'

Gabble crept backwards, still gazing up at the blinding sky, now trying to keep both the kestrel and Na'dir in view. The other rat walked casually forwards, grinning at his intended victim.

'Just listen,' said Gabble, urgently. 'Please.'

But Na'dir, now in the centre of the clearing, gave a short laugh. He crouched, muscles bunching. The kestrel, silent, hung overhead. Gabble saw its head turn, fixing on the other rat. Paw over paw, he eased away until grass stems crushed against his back, and a shady fringe of green hung over his head. Then he too lowered himself down, coiled to spring.

Na'dir surveyed Gabble, contempt written across his face. 'Coward,' he jeered. 'Hide all you want; it won't help you.'

And Na'dir came for him. Gabble hurled himself backwards, tumbling bodily into the grasses, tail over feet. The world blurred in greens and stems as the tussock closed around him. But amidst the rustles and cracks Gabble heard a single, solid thump and a cry, cut short. He twisted to his feet, up and ready to run. Through the stems he clearly saw reddish feathers and spread wings as the kestrel danced and clawed at the ground. And then the wings folded. The kestrel turned its head, scanning the ground around it. For a terrifying instant its black eye fixed on Gabble's position. And then it leapt up, beating with its wings. As it took flight

Gabble glimpsed what it clutched, pulled up tight in its claws. And then bird and prey were gone from view. A dizzy, sick sensation overcame Gabble and he huddled down, breathing quick, shallow gulps of air.

'Gabble!' Feather's call was filled with panic. 'Gabble, where are you?'

Gabble tried to speak. He wanted to tell her that he was fine, to call her over. He wanted to put his paws around her, and hold her until his breathing calmed. But he could only sag into the tussock and curl up.

'Gabble?' She sounded closer now. And then paws were on his flanks, uncurling him. 'Are you all right?'

He looked up into Feather's worried face. He reached out and grasped her fur, eyes squeezed shut and waiting for the hurt and the fear to ebb. Feather's fur was soft, and filled with the warm scent of home. She smelled of the burrow, the familiar scents that spoke of his Mothers and his puphood. And somehow, in some way that he couldn't explain, it felt right to be there, holding her. Her presence washed over Gabble, calming him, bringing him round.

'I'm sorry,' said Gabble. 'I—'

'It's all right,' she said. 'It's OK.' She waited, head against his, until his shaking had stopped. And then, gently, she let him go. She stepped away, head on one side.

'You stink,' she said, but gave him a small smile. She cleared her throat. 'You'd better groom that off.' Then she turned to watch something across the clearing and frowned. 'And then I'm going to need you to answer two questions.'

'Questions?' said Gabble.

Feather nodded. 'Yes. Mostly, where have you been all this time?' Then she nodded past Gabble's shoulder and her eyes glinted, stonily. 'But first I'd like to know who *they* are, and whether they really want to fight me.'

Gabble, muzzy and confused, followed Feather's gaze. Across the clearing, breathing hard, stood Na'dir's two companions, Piebald and Cringer. They sidled uncertainly. Gabble grasped at grass stems and wrestled free from the tussock's embrace. Then he took two wobbly steps into the clearing, and faced them, swaying.

'Where's Na'dir?' asked Cringer. 'I smell him.'

'Na'dir's with the Taker. Heh. I warned him not to fight me. But he didn't listen.' Gabble watched the rats' faces carefully. They exchanged uncertain glances, staring about them. Na'dir's final scent, of terrified, hurt rat, still hung in the clearing.

'Go back to your clan,' Gabble told them. 'Tell them what happened here. Tell them what happens when the Chosen leave the Damplands.'

Piebald raised his chin. 'Too late for that. The Chosen are gathering.' He turned an eye to the clearing, taking in the disturbed grasses and Feather's large frame.

'We'll go back. And we'll tell Rai'thir of your betrayal. But you'll see us again,' he said. Then the rats turned and were gone.

Gabble hunched down against the ground, breathing deeply and wishing it all away. He hadn't saved Ash. He hadn't stopped the Damplanders. Visions filled his mind, of the Mothers driven out, of the Greenhedge ransacked. And with the visions came anger that clenched his muscles still tighter. All the promises he had made; were they just words that meant nothing, changed nothing? He had broken all of them. *What good are words, Trickster, if they can't change rats' thoughts? What good is your dance, if no rats follow?* Gabble shook his head, trying to shake away the bitter thoughts. Perhaps this world was not a world in which his words or actions could make a difference. Well, he would see the next world soon enough. And there he would stand before the Taker and speak his truth. *I am Fo'dur and I earned my name with words.*

Gabble's breath caught in his throat. *I earned my name with words.* Where had that thought come from? He came to his feet, wild-eyed.

'It's about names,' he said. 'Of course it is. Heh.' He staggered about to face Feather. 'I mean, I knew names were important. But I hadn't realized . . .' He broke off. 'All of us have a true name. Each and every rat. It's who we are. It's how we live. It's how we earn it, and keep earning it. And that's what we bring to the Taker. I'll take my name to him, and show him a rat who lived the best he could, who was true to himself, and earned his name with words.' He grinned, stupidly. 'Words that dance.'

'Gabble,' interrupted Feather, 'those rats just said there are Damplanders coming. Lots of Damplanders. You need to stop babbling and we need to go.'

'I can't stop,' said Gabble with a grin. 'Babbling is what Gabble does. Because that's his name. But I have another name too. It's Fo'dur. And I earned it from the Trickster.'

'What are you talking about?'

'Names, don't you see? Ash took mine and thought it was his. He's trying to live the wrong name. And it won't work.'

Feather backed away, shaking her head. Gabble pattered after her. 'Listen to me,' he insisted. 'The Damplanders are coming because they want their names. They're nameless because they don't have enough rats to fight. They think Ash will give them what they want, but he can't. They're a clan of bullies and drudges who think they're Chosen but know they're lost. And they'll follow Ash because he's the nearest thing they have to hope. But that hope is a lie.' Gabble's voice was hoarse as the words poured from him. 'And all because they're following the wrong name.'

Two paws grabbed hold of him and yanked him upright. He found himself hoisted half off the ground, staring directly into Feather's face. 'Will you get a grip on yourself?' she demanded.

'Heh. Looks like you've done it for me.'

'Listen, stupid,' Feather hissed. 'The Damplanders are coming. Right now. What are we going to do?'

'Good question.' Gabble grinned at her. Then he widened his eyes, staring over her shoulder. 'Look out—the kestrel!'

Feather's head jerked around. In an instant Gabble twisted free of her grip. She rounded on him with a scowl. He held up a paw.

'Sorry, but you were hurting me and I needed you to let go.' He gave her a smile. 'But I know what I have to do. And if it works everything will be saved.'

'What if it doesn't?'

'Can things get worse? But I have three clans to save, and a brother who's living the wrong name. And I can sort it all out. I can.'

He looked at Feather's expression—angry, exasperated, and worried—and an odd, warm feeling crept into his heart. He felt as though he could curl up with her, and sleep safe while he healed. And somehow he thought that she might like that too, and that thought made him happy. But he couldn't. Not yet. First the Trickster had work for him.

'Don't look so worried,' he said. 'I know what I'm going to do.'

She gave him a suspicious look. 'And what's that, exactly?'

'Heh. I'm going to get my name back.'

chapter twelve

Gabble's chin knocked against cold metal. The impact was gentle but it brought his head up. He clawed free of the sleep that clutched at him. *Come on, come on, what sort of rat are you?* Sleep must wait. He had words to spin, a dance to lead, a name to win, and a brother to save. *The Shining One. Heh. That's no name for a rat who can't stay awake.*

The moon was high, flooding the grassy margin with light. He crouched lower, merging with the moon-shadows at the top of his refuge. He didn't want to be seen. Not yet. Beneath him the heap of tangled metal still enclosed the hollow where, days before, he had cringed, sheltering from the cat. He gazed down the verge to the Damplands. This was the closest point of the margin to the henburrow, as good a place to make a stand as any, and better than most. Not that this ramshackle cage could protect him from the Damplanders. But if Feather had done her job then hopefully it wouldn't have to. He wished that she were here. *Strange. Heh*. But she had gone to the Greenhedge to speak with her father, the Bossrat. Gabble had told her what he wanted, and for once she hadn't argued. But before she left, she had smiled an odd smile and laid a mark, soft as her namesake, on his flank. The memory stirred in him, making him half proud, half sad. He shook his head. No time for that, either. If things went badly he would find himself in the Land of Bones, handing his name to the Taker. But at least he would have done his best. And surely that was all any of them, Mother, Hunter, Trickster, or Taker, could ask.

The pile of twining grass and metal seemed to lurch and shift beneath his weight. He blinked at it. No. It hadn't moved. He had drifted off again. He lifted a paw and watched it shake. 'Heh,' he said, and placed it back. He had found a scatter of grass seeds and a gulp of water at the base of the tower, but they had done little to quell the tremors that ran through his body. He was nothing but bones and bruises, scabs, fur, aches, and smothering fatigue. And words, always those.

He lifted his whiskers to the breeze. The air was cold, and he pulled it deep into his chest to chase the drowsiness away. And as he did, a scent floated to him.

It flowed into his senses, his mind, his heart, and blood. It brought fear and a final surge of strength. It twitched his ears up and sharpened his gaze, fixing them on the verge. Seen from above, the grasses swayed and moved, straight lines and pulses that ran back and forth, back and forth as wave after wave of unseen rats ran towards Gabble's tower. So this was it. The Damplanders had come.

It would be the drudges first: the dead, the nameless. Send out the most desperate. Send out the ones for whom hope burned the strongest. And then the first few Bigrats, with Ash in their ranks, protected. Last would be Rai'thir, safe in the body of his clan. That was how the Damplanders were. And now, among the grasses, Gabble could glimpse individual rats; here a nose, there a glimmer of coat or tail. Not yet. Not yet. Wait until they are almost at the tower. Make an impression.

Now.

Gabble hauled and scrabbled to the highest point, a rusted metal spur that glinted dully in the moonlight. His heart surged, pulsing blood to his claw tips. He stretched to his full height, and held himself there. The moon caught his belly fur, his whiskers, his eyes, glinting and reflecting from his outstretched paws. He glanced at his fur, shining silver in the brightmoon. *Heh. That'll make an impression.*

'Rats, hear me!'

The movements below became a muddle and tumble as the Damplanders at the front stopped, and those behind pressed forward. Rats stood, rising up from the grass, staring, gesturing and chattering. The wave of Damplanders broke, washing back from the base of Gabble's tower. Forelegs still outstretched, he watched them. Spreading as far back as he could see, the grass was rippling with rats. He should be terrified, but somehow he was not. Not while he had words to speak.

'Hear me!' he yelled again. 'I want to talk to your Shining One. Bring him out.'

A murmur ran through the assembled rats. Gabble saw heads turning, seeking Ash. Then Gabble ducked out of the moonlight, jumping back into the shadow, deep in the structure of the tower. He clung to the metal, panting, and listened to the confusion of the Damplanders below. They could scale the frame and drag him down, and then Gabble would be done for. But these were the nameless, and Ash was guiding them, they thought, to their names. They would do nothing without him. Gabble crept to a hole in the metal, and settled down to watch. Rats were pattering to and fro. Some ran back, no doubt to fetch the Bigrats, and some sniffed at the base of the metal, and flinched away. But eventually the milling forms parted around a small group of larger shapes that marched through them. Within that group Gabble caught a flash of white. His breath quickened. It was Ash, unmistakable even amidst the silver-splashed grasses. He dragged himself back up onto his metal outcrop, where the moonlight painted him white.

'There!' Gabble shouted. 'There! I see him! I challenge him. I challenge your Shining One to fight me for my name.'

He heard angry mutters from the Bigrats and they surged forwards, running for the tower. They glared up, eyes shining and paws on the metal, ready to swarm up and take Gabble right there.

'No! Stop.' A hacking cough and a hoarse shout. 'You lot . . . don't move. I need to talk to him.' It was Ash's voice. The Bigrats shrank back and stood reluctantly aside as Ash laboured to the base of the metal.

'What are you doing, Gabble?' he croaked.

'I'm challenging you,' Gabble shouted back. 'I want to honour the Taker, and fight you for my name.'

Ash's ears went flat. 'I was given this name by the Taker himself,' he yelled. 'He touched me . . . he named me!' Ash panted with the effort, breath rasping and bubbling.

Gabble smiled. 'Then we will honour him more in our fight, won't we?'

'You don't know what you're doing,' said Ash. Red

tears trickled from his eyes and nose. He wiped at them, and held up his paws. 'Gabble, look at me,' he said, and now his voice was almost pleading. 'I'm the Shining One. Don't do this.'

Gabble drew a shaky breath, but swallowed his pity. He had a job to do. 'All I see is a rat who's refusing me the chance of a name. I see a rat who won't fight.' Gabble mocked his brother in front of the Damplanders. 'You want to lead rats to their names, heh? So start here. Give me mine.'

The muttering from among the rats rose in pitch, angry and confused, but calmed as Ash rose up on his haunches.

'Fo'dur is my name,' said Ash. 'Mine.'

'Then prove it,' called Gabble.' He gestured to the Notratlan stone. 'There. Now. Come and fight me for it.'

Ash shook his head. But, Gabble knew, surrounded by Damplanders, that he had no choice.

'All right,' said Ash. 'We'll fight.'

Gabble nodded once. 'Good,' he said. Then he dropped back into the shadows and began picking his way down the metal frame. It took everything he had just to keep from falling.

Gabble's legs got him to the grass. He felt it beneath his feet, and against his whiskers. He felt the edge of the soil, then stone, cold on his paws. He felt the eyes of countless Damplanders, watching as he walked out into Notratlan. His chin came up in response, showing them the strong rat, the challenger. *Move smoothly, don't stumble. Just these final steps.* When he was far enough he turned, and waited for his brother. At the edge of the verge the Damplander Bigrats gazed balefully out at him. The sight filled Gabble with grim satisfaction. They wanted to attack, to punish him for challenging their Shining One. But they couldn't. Their way was to fight, and so to honour the Taker. Ash would have to face him. And when he did . . . no. Don't think it. Just trust that Feather had done what he asked.

White shimmered amidst the grasses and Ash stepped out, not even bothering to check the scents. He limped slowly to where Gabble waited, and drew to a stop a rat's length from his brother. He put his head on one side.

'Whatzit, Gabbley.'

'Whatzit, Ash.'

Neither moved. Neither reached out a paw.

'So you betrayed me,' said Ash, at last. 'I never thought you would.'

Gabble said nothing, gazing at Ash's face. *How had this happened, that he was standing here with Ash, ready to fight him in front of another clan?*

'So what now?' said Ash. 'Are we really going to do this?'

Gabble nodded.

'Hah. Some Gabble you are,' said Ash. 'Now you can't even talk.'

'Never could. Heh. Not so you'd listen.'

Ash stared. Then he gave a short bark of a laugh. 'That's true.'

An odd, twisted smile spread across Gabble's face. The strangest feeling crept over him. Here was the Ash whom he had known as a pup, Ash with the big mouth, grinning, eyes shining, who wouldn't listen and couldn't stop. Here was the Ash who had nearly died, who had lost everything and found a lie, Ash who had followed that lie, too far, even for him. And here was Ash, the enemy whom he had to fight, to save everything. All these were Ash, all the same rat. The smile faded from Gabble's lips.

'This time you have to listen,' said Gabble. 'This time I'm not Gabble. I'm Fo'dur, and I'm doing what is right.' He lowered himself, painfully, into a crouch. 'Ready?'

'Gabble—'

'I said, are you ready?'

The words rapped out and Ash flinched back. A moment's hurt in his eyes, and a flash of anger in return.

'Why are you doing this?' Ash demanded.

'Because one of us has to live our name.'

And Gabble hurled himself at his brother. He struck with both forepaws, as hard as he could. Ash, with no time to react, was caught, half up on his haunches. The impact snapped his head back and took him from his feet. And then Gabble was on him, binding with his forelegs, and wrestling him to the ground. Ash thrashed in his grip, flailing and snapping his teeth. But as injured and exhausted as Gabble was, he was still stronger. Ash twisted free for a moment, and rolled away. He tried to lunge, but his legs buckled. Gabble was up and attacking before Ash could take a step. Ash twisted onto his back, bringing his feet up, but now he was paddling, not attacking but fending Gabble off. He coughed and hacked, and his movements grew nervous and twitchy. Gabble smashed past Ash's defences and grabbed him, holding him with ease. Ash's eyes swivelled and his paws flailed. His breathing became quick and shallow. His mouth jerked open as though he would speak. And then his eyes closed, and he breathed out in a rattling sigh. Ash went limp, and slumped sideways.

Gabble straightened, releasing his grip. Part of him was horrified, hoping that Ash was all right. The rest was up and alert, watching the verge. The fight was done, and he had won. But the Damplanders would never let it go at that. They needed their Shining One.

And, sure enough, Damplander Bigrats were stepping hesitantly from the grasses onto the Notratlan stone.

'I have defeated this rat and claimed my name,' Gabble yelled. 'And now I tell you that this is not your place.' Even at this distance he could see the doubt in the Damplanders' eyes. *That's right*, he thought, *remember the fear*. 'Go home, Chosen. This is Notratlan and it is cursed.'

The Damplanders lingered uncertainly at the verge. Maybe, just maybe, they would leave. Perhaps it really could be this easy. But then a group of Bigrats began to advance. Gabble swore under his breath. He grabbed Ash's fur with his forepaws and strained with his back, tugging at his brother's inert body. Ash's head began to drag and bounce across the ground. Gabble's muscles burned, and the skin on his back felt as though it were tearing afresh, but each heave drew Ash closer to the henburrow.

A cry went up from among the Damplanders, and their Bigrats surged forwards; not many, but enough. They came with a rush and a pause, their gazes darting from shadow to shadow, and their whiskers stiff and twitching. Gabble, still working at Ash, watched them. They were afraid of Notratlan, but they were furious. He was taking their Shining One. And behind them lurked rank after rank of the nameless, also angry and bewildered. Gabble redoubled his efforts, trying in vain to drag Ash to the henburrow, but he knew it was pointless. The attackers were coming too quickly. He filled with bitter thoughts. He had relied on Feather. He had needed everything to be ready. But it had gone wrong, and now he was on his own.

The lead Damplander sidled forwards, stopping just beyond striking distance. Behind him Gabble spied Piebald and Cringer. So they too had come for their names. Gabble released Ash and raised his paws, ready to fight but knowing he would lose. *I have a name for the Taker*, Gabble thought, *but I didn't want to need it yet*.

'I defeated him,' said Gabble. 'But that doesn't matter, does it? Because you need Ash. Because if you let him go then your clan will have lost its Shining One.' He shook his head. 'So much for your honour.'

The lead Damplander shifted, but lifted his chin. Then his eyes locked onto something beyond Gabble, deep in the Notratlan shadows. Steps pounded on stone and rats hurtled past, smashing bodily into the Damplanders. The leader was sent sprawling to the floor. He rolled up and then fell back, squeaking, as an immense, scarred shape leapt for him. It was Ar'bus, head and whiskers outlined in silver and a savage grin on his face. He lunged again, teeth flashing, and the Damplander went down with a cry. And then the old rat was away, diving for the group containing Cringer. To Gabble's left, Shrill was rolling and biting, fighting

Piebald, and beyond him was Snip, jumping and twisting and striking at a big male. A Damplander grabbed for Gabble, who wrenched away, then stumbled, and fell beneath its weight. He scrabbled and struggled, trying to evade its teeth. The next instant it was gone, flung aside, and paws were tugging at Gabble's fur, bringing him to his feet. He found himself facing Snip who winked at him, then leapt at the nearest Damplander. Spinning about, Gabble spied Shrill, still battling Piebald, but on his back and desperately fending with his paws. He sprinted to Shrill's side, and slammed his weight into Piebald, sending him tumbling away. Shrill climbed to his feet as Piebald staggered into the path of Ar'bus, and was grappled to the ground.

But now more Damplanders were running from the grass, racing to help their clanmates. Gabble's heart lurched as he turned to face them. Shrill raised his chin, glaring out at the new attackers.

'I calls the cat on you! I do it. I calls the cat!'

His yell echoed across the stone and the advancing rats paused, eyes darting to Notratlan's shadows. And for an instant the fighting Damplanders hesitated. Ar'bus seized the opportunity, his teeth closing on the flank of Piebald, who let out a terrible scream and wrenched away before fleeing, shrieking, towards the oncoming Damplanders. Cringer fell back, unable to defend against Snip's lunges, then turned and ran.

And Snip and Gabble faced down a Damplander Bigrat, landing a blow on his muzzle that made him whimper, and clutch at his nose. And when Shrill bit his leg the Damplander fled, mewling. And with that the fight was over. Every Damplander was either down and unmoving, or sprinting for the safety of the verge. Their advancing clanmates joined the dash for cover. The Notratlan stone fell quiet. But the grasses of the verge seethed.

Gabble scurried to where Ar'bus and Snip were standing by Ash's prone form. He grabbed for Ash, meaning to drag him to safety, but Ar'bus shoved him away. 'Get to the henburrow,' Ar'bus ordered. 'We've got this one.'

Gabble caught Ar'bus's eye, unwilling to leave his brother.

'Move!' Ar'bus shouted. 'Those rats won't stay there for long. More will come.' He took hold of Ash. Snip and Shrill joined him, and together they began yanking Ash to safety. Gabble nodded once, then limped and gasped his way to the shelter of the henburrow wall. He huddled there, barely able to stand, watching for danger. And now Ash was at the entrance and Ar'bus and Snip were shoving him bodily beneath the wooden slats. Ar'bus dived inside, and Snip crowded after. Gabble lurched his way down the wall to the entrance, where Shrill was waiting. He drew to an uncertain halt, facing the other rat.

'Whatzit,' said Gabble.

'You helped Shrill.'

Gabble nodded.

Shrill thought for a second then said, 'I call the cat on them?'

Gabble eyed him uncertainly, wondering if the cat could drive the Damplanders away. But, even if it did, Hope might be in those grasses. And other rats too, whose only crime was to follow their Akla. It might kill them. He shook his head. 'Heh. Maybe next time.'

Shrill nodded solemnly. Then his face split into a grin, and he clapped a paw on Gabble's shoulder. 'When you need it I call it, right?'

Gabble returned the smile weakly, and together they watched the verge grasses, filled with the Damplanders' scurryings. He wondered how many rats there were, and how many more would come. He wondered if he had done enough to stop them. Perhaps. He had, after all, defeated their Shining One. But Rai'thir was coming, and Gabble remembered Hope's expression when she had thought of gaining her name, and the smell of desperation in the Damplander's burrow. And these memories filled him with unease.

Gabble nodded to Shrill and then crept beneath the wooden slats. He stumbled into the gloom, and followed the path up through the henburrow to Ar'bus's chambers.

CHAPTER THIRTEEN

Ar'bus and Gabble stood side by side, gazing down at Ash. The henburrow was oddly quiet, as though even the chickens had sensed the events of the night, and were keeping a muted vigil. On Ar'bus's orders Snip and Shrill had gone to watch for the Damplanders. And now he and Gabble stood by Ash as he lay on the floor, neck stretched out and eyes closed. In the quiet Gabble could hear the breath in his brother's chest, a faint crackle, just at the edge of hearing.

'I know what you want me to do,' said Gabble at last. 'But I can't.'

'He's dangerous, Gabble,' said Ar'bus.

'He's my brother.'

'If he walks from this chamber he'll go back to them. Nothing will change. Our victory will be for nothing.'

Ar'bus's face was grim. 'You don't want that, lad.'

Gabble's jaw clenched and unclenched. He couldn't do what Ar'bus wanted. He was no Damplander. He would not end his brother's life. Ever so gently, Gabble eased down beside Ash, and laid his paws on his brother's fur. He rested there, cuddled against him. Somewhere beneath the layers of Rai'thir's scent was a hint of Ash's own smell. Working gently, Gabble began to groom his fur, stripping Rai'thir away. Bent to his labour, he did not look up at Ar'bus.

'You're right,' said Gabble. 'I don't want Ash to go back to the Damplanders. And he won't. But I can't let you hurt him. Not when there's another way.'

'Gabble,' said Ar'bus. 'I—'

'Ar'bus.' Gabble fought to keep his voice level. 'I said I owed you a debt, and I'm repaying it the only way I know how. Let me do it. Just find Feather. She should be here with two Hunters. Let them come and it will all be right. I promise.'

'Very well,' said Ar'bus, stiffly. Gabble heard him turn to leave. 'I expected better of you.' His paws pattered away into the burrow.

Fatigue washed through Gabble, but he kept his paws moving, working down Ash's flank and burrowing through the scents to the rat he wanted his brother to be. Ash stirred and red trickled from his eyes and nose. Then his head lolled onto the floor. Gabble sighed, but kept going. Even here Rai'thir's scent was strong. Gabble couldn't tell if he was making a difference. But he had to do something. After what seemed an age he heard the approach of rats. He raised his head.

'Feather, are you there? Did you bring them?'

He heard a quiet scuffle in the shadows, and Feather approached.

'Yes, they're here,' she said. 'Are you OK?'

Gabble couldn't answer that question. 'Thank you,' he whispered. Then he raised his voice. 'Hello, Mothers.'

From behind Feather two rats stepped out. They moved cautiously, hesitantly, not knowing what they would find. Gabble stepped away from Ash's body. He could not bring himself to meet their eyes, but he knew without looking it was them. Their way of breathing and their warm scent filled him with memories of a home that seemed unbearably distant.

'I'm sorry,' said Gabble, talking to the ground. 'He's alive, and he's still Ash. But he's lost his way. He's nameless, though he doesn't know it. He took my name for his own. I would have shared it with him.' He swallowed against a sudden sorrow. 'But it wasn't enough. Nothing ever is for him. Bustle, Whisker, I'm so sorry. I promised to protect him. I couldn't.' Then Gabble turned and bowed his head to Whisker. 'Na'sta. Mother. I am your Fo'dur. And I have failed you. Both of you.'

His eyes filled with tears. He groomed them away with a paw. The Mothers still did not speak, their eyes lingering on Ash.

'I wanted you here, Bustle, to give Ash his name. He didn't hear it when you told him before. He's been living the wrong life.'

Bustle hesitated. She looked questioningly at Whisker who nodded. 'I think you should,' she said. Then she moved to stand in front of Gabble, eyes searching his face. Finally she said, 'You didn't fail us. You did everything you promised and more.'

Gabble hung his head, trying not to cry. From behind him he heard Ash's breathing change. Paws paddled and scraped at the dusty wood floor as Ash heaved himself upright. His head swayed as he focused on the assembled rats.

'Gabble?' Ash blinked. 'Mothers. I—I don't understand. What's going on?' And something in his voice was different. The strange note it had held, arrogant and brittle, was gone. He sounded more like Ash; hurt and broken, but Ash.

Gabble rushed to his side. 'It's easy, Ash. It's so easy. We're in the henburrow. And outside are the Damplanders. Some of them want to fight, to spill blood. But most of them just want their names. They want a quick victory so they can find burrows, sleep in nests, look for food and raise children. They want a name to live, and to give to the Taker when they die.' The words came tumbling from Gabble's mouth as he clutched for his brother, holding him tight. 'But some of them will fight, Ash, because they think they have to. And the Damplanders will win and then they will go to the Greenhedge, and our clan will die, trying to defend their own pups and brothers. And all because of Rai'thir. And because of you.' Gabble took a breath and held Ash to him. 'Oh, Ash. Is this really what you want? It can't be, can it?'

Gabble squeezed his eyes shut. Like this he could pretend that everything was how it should be: just he and Ash, together, curled like pups. All he had to do was keep his eyes closed tight and the world could be anything that he wanted. Ash held on to Gabble for a moment, but then gently pushed free. Gabble opened his eyes. And there he was, Rai'thir's Shining One, with his eyes and nose crusted dark red, grazes covering his flank, and his white fur stained and mottled from being dragged across Notratlan. He looked like the most miserable rat Gabble had ever seen. From nowhere a laugh bubbled out of Gabble. Ash stiffened.

'I don't see what's funny.'

'Look at the state of us.' Gabble couldn't tell whether he was laughing or crying. 'I'm sure the Mothers are appalled.'

Ash raised his eyes to Gabble's face and then looked

at the Mothers. A rueful expression stole over his features.

'Yep, they look it. But nothing new there. Appalling the Mothers is what I'm best at.' Then he fixed his red eyes on Gabble's face. 'But why are they here?'

Bustle stepped forwards. 'We're here because Gabble asked us to be. We came to give you your name.'

Ash's eyes went hard. 'My name?'

'Yes, Ash,' said Gabble. 'I told you. Fo'dur is *my* name.'

Whisker stepped forwards. 'Ash, it's true. Fo'dur is the name I gave to Gabble. It wasn't meant for you.'

Silence filled the chamber. Ash looked from rat to rat, as if seeking an escape. They met his gaze with solemn faces. His whiskers began to tremble. He groomed them to stillness. He swallowed.

'I see,' he said. He took a breath and raised his eyes to the darkness above. For long moments he did nothing but stare away. Then he shook his head. 'I saw him you know, Gabble. The Taker. I did. I heard his voice, so clearly. And I thought I was doing what he wanted, and living as I should. You know, like I always said.' He laughed, gently. 'Didn't work, did it?'

'Not really.'

Bustle pattered forwards, and stopped a short distance from Ash.

'You are my son and I gave you your name. I can give it to you again, if you would like. If you'll let me?'

Ash went stiff. He barely breathed. 'My name,' he murmured. Then he nodded, barely perceptibly. 'Yes,' he said softly. 'Please. I'd like to know it.'

Bustle lowered her lips to Ash's ear, and spoke in a whisper. She pressed her paws to his flank, then bowed her head and stepped away. A faltering smile appeared on Ash's face.

'Ah,' he said. 'I see.' Then he clambered to his feet, swaying on the spot. He stretched his legs out, wincing at his pulling muscles. Then he nodded to Bustle. 'Good name, that.' He turned to Gabble, head on one side. 'All right,' he said. 'It looks like I have to give you this one, Gabbley. But don't think you'll always be right. OK?'

Then Ash closed his eyes. A single tear, clear as spring water, trickled down his cheek. 'Gabble, I'm sorry. It was so confused, you know?' Ash rapped the side of his head with a paw. 'In here. And while I was saying things and rats were listening I thought I had it sorted. I thought I could do something . . . good. I thought that was what I was meant to do. But it wasn't. And it's a mess, isn't it?'

'Yes,' said Gabble, earnestly. 'But we can make it right. Together.'

Ash stared. Then burst out laughing. His breath came in giant whoops as he hunched over, shaking. Eventually the laughter subsided.

'Oh, I needed that,' said Ash. 'Gabble, you'll never change. Even after all this you're trying to look after me. Go on then. I'll let you. If you tell me it'll be all right I'll believe you.' He gave Gabble a strange look, amused, but desperate. And filled with hope. 'So do it. Tell me how we sort it out.'

'We leave,' said Gabble. 'You and me. We'll go somewhere else. And without their Shining One maybe the Damplanders will go home.'

Ash shook his head. 'No. Won't work. Sorry. The Chosen aren't going anywhere. You fought off the first of them, but Rai'thir's coming with more rats. And they need their names.' He gazed at his brother. 'A rat can't live without a name, Gabble. I know that better than most. They've been promised names, and they'll stay until they get them.' He straightened, and his eye glinted, dangerously. 'This has to stop here. I need to go out there.'

Gabble shook his head, but Ash cut across him.

'Not this time. This time you're wrong and I'm right.'

'That's what you always think,' said Gabble.

Ash didn't smile. 'True.' Then he took a step forwards and took Gabble in his paws. He pulled him tight. 'You're my brother and I love you,' said Ash. 'You've done your bit, and now it's my turn. I can sort this, but I need you to make me a promise.'

'What promise?'

'Get me out there, and let me do my thing. But don't look after me any more.'

'But—'

'Gabble, it's time to let go. Please. I know my name, and that tells me what I need to do. I won't let you down. Not this time.' Gabble opened his mouth, but Ash whispered. 'I swear by your name, Fo'dur. I'll be worthy of you. I will.' Then Ash smiled. 'Besides, I'm not a running-away kind of a rat.' He nodded at Bustle. 'She can tell you why.'

Gabble nodded miserably. He had no choice. 'All right. I promise.'

Ash pulled back and held Gabble at paw's length. 'Good rat.' Then he grinned. 'Right. I've had enough of being serious. It's not good for me.' He nudged Gabble's shoulder. 'Ack, don't look so worried. It's not like any of us will meet the Taker alive.' Then he turned, and faced the Mothers. He bowed to them, then winked and went to the entrance of the chambers. He set off, walking slowly but purposefully down the tunnel towards the entrance to Notratlan.

Feather joined Gabble. 'What's he doing?' she whispered.

'Being Ash. As hard as he can,' Gabble replied. And then he followed Ash, down the tunnel to the threshold of the world outside.

*

The moon was shining brightly when Ash walked from the henburrow. He did not stop to check for danger but simply staggered out across the stone. Gabble made to follow him, but Ash turned, a smile twitching in his whiskers.

'You promised, remember?' he said. 'You said you'd let me go.'

'Yes, but—'

'Now's the time. Notratlan's no place for a rat like you. Wait here, and keep your promise.' Then he set off.

Gabble watched him, an unhappy feeling rising in his throat. He didn't know what Ash was planning, only that now, at last, he was going where Gabble could not follow.

'What are you doing?' The words roared from further down the henburrow wall. Gabble spun to see Ar'bus sprinting towards him, Snip and Shrill scampering in his wake. Ar'bus skidded to a stop, glaring.

'You let him go?' he yelled. '*This* was your idea?' He tensed, as though he would hurl himself after Ash and drag him back to the henburrow. Gabble grabbed for Ar'bus.

'Leave him alone,' Gabble hissed. 'This isn't your business.'

'It's my clan.' Ar'bus's voice was dangerously quiet.

'And it's my brother,' Gabble returned. 'And he's

going there to save your clan.' He released his hold on Ar'bus. 'Now, fight me, or help me, but don't you touch Ash. He's gone beyond you. Understand?'

'You stupid Hunter,' said Ar'bus. 'The Damplanders are still there! That's what I came to tell you. And their Akla has come. We saw him with all his Bigrats. You've just given them the one thing they need.'

'Rai'thir's there, yes. Ash said he was coming,' said Gabble, quietly. 'And I'm not a Hunter, I'm a Trickster. Tricksters know about words, and we know how they bind us. I told you that I would pay my debt,' he nodded after Ash, 'and Ash told me that he would pay his. I promised to let him go, and I'm going to keep that promise. Even if it means fighting you.'

Ar'bus glared, muscles bunching as though ready to attack. Gabble stared back, defiantly.

'Trickster, is it?' said Ar'bus.

'That's right. Heh.'

And then, unexpectedly, Ar'bus's lips twitched to a smile. He gave a great shout of laughter. 'Hah! What does it matter?' He grinned as though he had gone mad. 'If they attack we fight or we run. Either way we're done for. May as well give him his chance.'

Ar'bus turned to watch Ash's laboured progress across the stone. Shrill and Snip exchanged looks, then moved up to stand beside him. Feather too stepped from the shelter of the henburrow, and came closer to

Gabble. She pressed next to him, her presence warm and reassuring.

'Lucky for him he didn't try to fight you,' she whispered, glowering meaningfully at Ar'bus.

Despite everything, her words gave Gabble a small surge of warmth. He smiled at her. 'Right. Heh.'

Feather thumped Gabble's shoulder. 'I meant it.'

'I know.'

Ash reached the centre of Notratlan. His fur glimmered in the full moonlight, and the dark stains beneath his eyes were black as a burrow. The verge edges rustled with Damplanders, bustling forwards, surging to the limits of their refuge. Countless pairs of eyes reflected red then blinked out: rats peeking from between the stems before scurrying back. Ash swayed slightly on the spot, watching them with interest. Then he grinned. Gabble saw his lips move, and the breeze fetched his words to the henburrow. *This looks like fun.*

Then Ash raised his voice. 'Chosen!' he shouted. 'I want to talk to you.' A murmur ran through the waiting rats. Something was happening. 'I am the one you call Fo'dur, the Shining One. I'm your sign from the Taker. I will lead you to your names. Isn't that right?'

A sound rippled through the Damplanders: half agreement, half expectation. Eyes locked hungrily on Ash's thin form.

'So I'm here to do what was promised,' he shouted.

'I'll give you your names, and all you need is the courage to take them.'

Next to Gabble, Ar'bus and Feather tensed. A word from Ash could send the Damplanders towards them. Ash gestured back at the henburrow.

'But you won't find your names in there,' he called. 'You might kill another rat, and your Akla might be pleased, but that doesn't make you brave. It means you're lost.' Ash raised his voice, shouting against an angry mutter. 'If you want your names I can tell you where they are: they're back in your clanlands. Rai'thir took them from you when you were born. He holds them in his burrow. He has them because you are scared.' Ash's eyes glittered in the moonglow. 'You're scared of him and of his Bigrats, and so your names are his, to give back if he wants.' Ash shook his head. 'Your most precious gift and you let a rat like that take it from you. A rat who cringes in the dark and sends you to fight in his place.'

Gabble heard discontent among the Damplanders. There was outrage from the Bigrats, but below that was a different tone. It ran deeper, and it came from the nameless ones. But even as the anger swelled a disturbance ran through their ranks. Rats hurried aside as a colossal form shouldered through them. Gabble's breath caught as the breeze carried the newcomer's scent to his nostrils. A familiar odour, pungent and powerful, flowed across Notratlan. Feather stiffened. Ar'bus growled, low in his throat. Gabble groomed the smell from his whiskers with his paws, but still it remained.

'Is that their Akla?' Feather whispered.

'Yes. Heh,' said Gabble, grimly. 'That's Rai'thir.'

Gabble could see the faces poking from between the grasses. The Bigrats' expressions were vivid with triumph, and they barged through the nameless to cluster around their Akla. But other rats were grudging, shooting sullen, resentful glances at Rai'thir. *These other rats had been hoping it would end*, Gabble thought. *They want to be at home in their burrows. And Rai'thir's presence means they must fight.* He scanned the faces, looking for Hope. He wondered if she was in there, whether she was all right.

Rai'thir carved his path to the very front of the ranks of his Chosen. His coat was glossy and his gigantic frame lush with muscles. He stood head and shoulders above even the Bigrats that flocked to him. He gazed stonily out at Ash, head and ears up. And Ash, tiny by comparison, didn't appear even slightly worried. He simply waited for the stir among the Damplanders to die.

'Oh look, it's Rai'thir.' He grinned. 'Now that's an unexpected revulsion. I didn't think you'd be brave enough to talk to me.'

'You accuse me, and I answer,' said Rai'thir. He raised his forepaws. 'You see me, my Chosen. I do not cringe in my burrow. I have come to my beloved clan. I have come to see you named.'

Gabble heard the smooth quality of Rai'thir's voice. He saw the heads of the Damplanders turn to him. He saw rats nodding.

'Your beloved clan?' Ash scoffed. 'Shall I tell your *beloved* what you've done to them?' He gestured at Rai'thir. 'This rat stole your names and called you nameless. He made you kill and told you that you were honouring the Taker. And to these he gave a name. But your names were never his to take. They are part of you. They're who you are.' Ash's breath rasped, but he kept on talking. 'And the only way any rat honours the Taker is by having the courage to live their name.'

Rai'thir's lip curled in a snarl. 'And now we see that you have betrayed us. It's you who lies. We honour the Taker. That is our way. We live without fear and send rats to him so he may rise again.' Rai'thir swept the Damplanders with his gaze.

'Live without fear?' Ash's voice was filled with derision. 'Now that's interesting. Because it looks to me like I'm the only one standing in Notratlan.' Ash came up onto his haunches. 'If being a named rat, Chosen, means living without fear why are you there, hiding in the grass? What are you scared of, Rai'thir?'

Rai'thir said nothing, but watched Ash with a considering look. And around Rai'thir a murmur, of mixed anger and agreement, rose from among the Damplanders.

'Why isn't your Akla talking to me face to face?' Ash continued. 'If I'm lying why isn't he here, fighting me, proving me wrong? Eh, Rai'thir?'

Gabble felt Feather shift beside him, put a paw on his fur.

'Don't,' she whispered. 'Please.'

He realized that his muscles were tight, ready to run in, to drag Ash back. He remembered too clearly the feel of Rai'thir's paws in the dark, the rat's colossal strength. If Ash fought him he would be killed in an instant. But Gabble had promised. And also he wanted to stay near Feather, to protect her too. Caught by two duties, he forced himself to watch, to let Ash speak.

Rai'thir hesitated, eyes narrowed. He raised his muzzle and scented the night, scanning for danger. Ash was a dash away, across the stone. The huge rat could cover the ground easily, and Ash, weak and ill, would have no escape. And yet Rai'thir stayed where he was, safe with his clan.

'Come on, Rai'thir,' Ash mocked. 'You have your name, don't you? You can die and go to the world beyond. Nothing to worry about there.' Ash raised his chin. 'So come on out and we'll fight in the moonlight. It'll be fun.'

And now the eyes of the nameless were on Rai'thir.

'You are the Shining One,' said Rai'thir, smoothly. 'It would be dishonourable to fight you.'

And Ash laughed in Rai'thir's face. 'What a heap of cat dung!' he hooted. 'You can't have it both ways. Either I'm the Shining One, or I'm a liar. Either you won't fight or you're afraid to. Which is it?' Ash raised his nose to the breeze and drew down the scents. 'Oh, I can smell you. You do fear the Land of Bones. Even with all those rats' names to give the Taker, you're still a coward.'

The murmur among the watching rats grew to an angry chatter, whether directed at Rai'thir or Ash, Gabble could not tell. Rats were staring at Rai'thir and his Bigrats, nudging one another and gesturing. *They don't know*, Gabble thought. *They don't know who to believe.* He silently willed the nameless to see the truth, to turn against their Akla. And at that moment a voice called out from their ranks, shrill and loud, and filled with defiance and fear.

'He's right. The white rat's right.'

Rats' heads snapped around to see who had spoken. A small figure stepped from the grasses, the other side of Rai'thir from Ash. And Gabble felt his heart clench. This rat, standing on the Notratlan stone and defying her Akla, was Hope. Rai'thir's eyes blazed, fixed on her form. He nodded to a Bigrat, who slunk unnoticed into the grasses.

'He's right that Rai'thir stole our names,' Hope yelled, glaring over to where Rai'thir stood. 'But he can't have mine. Not any more. My mother named me in the nest, deep and secret where even Rai'thir couldn't hear.' And now her voice carried clearly in the hush that had fallen. 'My name is Do'than. Do you hear me, Rai'thir? I found it for myself and I'm earning it right now. I have killed no one, but still I earn my name. And that's why he's scared.' She raised her paws, pleading with the other rats. 'Are you listening? I'm telling you he's scared,' she shouted. 'He's scared because he knows you can have your names too, that you'll take them back. He's—'

Her words broke off in sharp squeak. A Bigrat had leapt from the dark and grasped her in its paws. She cried out and battled as she was borne down beneath its weight and then dragged, struggling, back from the moonlight and into the grasses. The other rats stood motionless as the grasses closed behind her, and her squeaks faded to silence. Gabble's gaze raked the place where Hope had been, desperately seeking any sign that she had escaped. But a deathly silence hung over Notratlan. Even Ash was staring at the grasses, momentarily unable to speak.

Gabble hung his head. 'They didn't help her,' he whispered. 'Look at them. Heh, they're just standing there.'

But Feather's grip on his shoulder tightened. 'No,' she said. 'Look.'

A ripple, of shock, or anger, ran through the nameless. Whispers passed between rats until the grasses rustled with disquiet. The sound ebbed and flowed around Rai'thir, before settling to a brooding calm. Gabble raised his head. He had heard a calm like this before. He had felt it in the henburrow, in the moments before the birds attacked. And now, in its wake, an upwelling of rage gathered, and broke out in an angry chatter, livid and resentful. Voices rose, directing fury at Rai'thir and his Bigrats. Fights erupted among the Damplanders, and the Bigrats were glaring, boxing and nipping at the rats around them, trying to keep the nameless at bay. But their actions only intensified the noise.

'Oh dear, Rai'thir,' Ash taunted, eyes shining. 'Your rats aren't too happy. And I can't blame them. I wouldn't want to be treated like that.' And now Ash's smile returned, scornful on his face. 'So come on, I'm waiting. Are you coming out here to fight, or are you going to send a Bigrat to do that for you too?'

Shouts, whistles, and furious squeaks almost drowned Ash's words. Rai'thir's head swivelled this way and that, seeking an escape from Ash's mockery and his clan's fury. But he found none. Ash and Hope between them had left him no choice. If he refused to face Ash everything he had ever told the Chosen would be shown to be hollow. And then, he knew, his clan would turn on him.

Rai'thir lifted his head. 'Very well,' he said. 'If you will have it so, then so it must be.'

The commotion died away as Rai'thir stepped out onto the stone. The hush gathered and deepened as he paced towards Ash, who stood unflinching at his approach. Ash turned, now grinning at the Damplanders, enjoying the trouble he had caused. The sight twisted in Gabble with a mix of joy and sorrow. This was the Ash he knew, doing what he did best, and enjoying every moment of it.

'Now there's a brave rat,' Ash called. 'That's more like it.' He glanced back to Gabble's small group, and raised a paw. Then Ash muttered something below his breath. Gabble thought he caught the words, *And now we'll see who fears the Taker*.

Ash waited until Rai'thir was a few, short lengths from where he stood, and then he stretched his muzzle to the sky.

'I hope you're ready for this, Rai'thir,' he said. 'Because I am. I always have been.' Then he raised his eyes to the sky and squeaked, high and clear, in a long call that echoed from the Notratlan stone.

And, as Ash drew a breath, an answering call sounded from the henburrow. Gabble spun, to see Shrill, his muzzle straining to the moon, yelling for his cat with everything he had. Ash whipped around, frowning. But when he saw Shrill he grinned, raised his face again and called out, in a long, pining note that echoed against Shrill's, over and over until it was impossible to hear where one began and the other ended. The rats in the verge stopped moving, whiskers and ears up, scanning for danger. Rai'thir too, stopped his advance, alert and listening. And again Ash yelled out, and again Shrill answered him. Over and over the two rats filled the air with their cat-calls. And Gabble realized, with a surge in his heart, that new cries had joined theirs, cries that came from the verge and rose up from the ranks of the nameless. More and more rats began to squeak and shout, and the din mounted. The nameless, led by Ash, poured their defiance up to the Taker's moon.

'What are they doing?' came Feather's voice, from beside Gabble. 'Gabble, what are they doing?' But Gabble did not answer. He took a hesitant step forwards, then stopped. He couldn't help. He had promised.

The noise was everywhere, almost too loud to bear. And in the centre of it stood two rats: Ash, crying out with everything he had, and Rai'thir, one paw lifted, eyes darting from rat to rat in the verge. Gabble saw the sinews straining in his brother's neck as Ash, summoning one final shout, collapsed, gasping, to all fours. And in that instant every cry ceased. The sound echoed on in the night, before dying away to nothing. And now the only noise was the crackling from Ash's chest as he dragged at the air while tears made red tracks down his face. And still Rai'thir stood there, one paw raised. The breeze blew softly, whispering in the grasses. It carried only Ash's laboured breathing. Everything else was still.

Then, around the henburrow corner, slunk a dark shape. The cat limped as it came, but its ears were pricked and its pace was eager. It wove a sinuous path along the wall, then stepped into the open. Its head swung as it ran, seeking the source of the call that had summoned it. The Damplanders spotted it, with terrified whispers and stifled cries. But then the cat spied the pair of rats, facing one another in the very centre of Notratlan. It stopped with a hiss and sank into a crouch, tail flicking. Its eyes were locked onto Ash and Rai'thir. Gabble could barely breathe. A dash and a lunge and it could take either. Rai'thir, watching its huge form, seemed frozen, motionless, but then he began, slowly and cautiously, to crouch. Muscles bunched beneath his fur as he readied himself to run. Ash turned to follow the direction of Rai'thir's gaze. He coughed and straightened, ears up.

'Ooh,' he said, 'we've got a cat. Now *that's* what I call fun.' He turned to Rai'thir. 'But which rat is it hunting, do you reckon? The small one, or the big one?' He blinked, an innocent look on his face. 'Shall we find out?'

Rai'thir began to shake. His paws trembled. His gaze never left the cat, and his breathing was shallow, fast. And then, moving almost imperceptibly slowly, he began to creep away, sidling for the verge. The cat focused on the movement. It sneaked forwards a pace, settled back over its paws. And in a rush it was on Rai'thir, and attacking. Rai'thir uttered a single, terrible scream as he rolled down beneath its weight. There was a confusion of raking claws and shrieks, and the cat skittered back a pace. In that instant Rai'thir was on his feet and fleeing for his life, head down and scurrying for the Damplands. The cat darted after him, pawing and leaping, trying to bring down its prey. Rai'thir dived for the grasses and disappeared. The cat jumped after him but lost its footing, rolling over in the grass. It came up and mewed in frustration, paws battering the ground in front of it.

'Hah!' Ash cried, exaltation written across his face. 'Hah! You see? You see?' he shouted. 'That was your Akla running away.' Ash began to cough, but he raised his voice still further. 'That coward was the rat who took your names. Him and these Bigrats.' Ash was choking and dragging at the air now, but still he kept shouting. 'Chosen, I . . . I promised you your names. Now's your time. Go and take them. Take them back from these cowards of rats!'

Jeers and shouts rang out from the Damplanders in the verge as the nameless turned on their Bigrats. Gabble watched in horrified fascination as the largest rats flailed, half hidden among the stalks, snarling and clawing at unseen ranks of smaller forms that flew at them, dragging them down amongst the stems. He glimpsed a piebald rat fighting clear before sprinting away. Then a Bigrat, and another, pelted crazily down the grasses, some limping and some squeaking in fear, but all fleeing the anger of their clan. And down the verge the cat waited, striking at any rat who came too close. It leapt and twisted, sending rats scrambling away. And only when the last of the Chosen was lost from sight did it turn, eyes gleaming, back to face Notratlan.

Rai'thir and his Bigrats were gone and now only the nameless remained, filling the night with their hushed rustling, their breathing, and the low squeaking of the injured. And in front of them all a lone white rat, still stood on his haunches, wheezing and laughing at the world. The cat's eyes fixed on Ash. It hunkered down low and began to inch forwards. Ash spotted it. He blinked. *Come on, Ash*, thought Gabble. *You've done everything you can. Now get back where it's safe.*

The cat eased closer. Ash stared at it, a strange smile on his face.

Please, Ash. Please come back.

But Gabble knew, with aching certainty, that Ash had truly gone beyond him. He saw his brother's smile broaden as he turned a final time to the Damplanders. Dark tears streamed down his cheeks. He dragged down a gasping breath that gurgled deeply within him. And he raised his voice a final time.

'Chosen, you have your names. You've earned them in the fight, and you'll find them in your hearts.' Ash gasped at the air. 'Now go home,' he cried. 'Go and live.'

The cat leapt. Unthinking, Gabble began to run, breaking his promise, and casting himself madly into Notratlan. But paws grabbed him from behind, bore him down and held him. Pinned immobile, but head up and reaching out for his brother, Gabble gazed across the stone. He could not bear to see where his brother had stood. Instead his eyes searched for anything that could help him, anything that was not death. The grasses reflected the moon in uncountable, broken dazzles that bobbed and weaved as the Damplanders scampered away. And there, at the very edge, was a single rat who was not running, but standing alone and looking back at him. As her gaze fastened on his, Gabble felt a jolt of recognition. She was far away, but he knew her. It was the rat who not long before had faced her Akla and claimed from him her name, Do'than—a name, that in Old Rat meant, simply, 'Hope'. A tremulous smile spread across her face. She lingered there as the lights danced around her. Then she bowed her head to him once, stepped back amongst the grasses, and was gone.

Gabble became aware of Feather's voice in his ear, urging and pleading. 'Gabble, you can't help him. Come back. Come on.'

He allowed himself to be brought to his feet. He glanced back at the grass, to the strange beauty of the dancing lights. But a cloud had passed across the moon, and the grasses were just grasses once more, mottled and greyish. Feather, though, her expression filled with worry, was luminous in his eyes. Gabble stared at her, while her paws shook him, insistent on his shoulders.

'. . . listening to me? Run, I said! Come on, move!'

Gabble pulled his attention from her face to her words. From somewhere he found the courage to ask what he needed to know. 'Ash. The cat?' Feather nodded, her eyes wide.

'Yes. I'm so sorry.'

Gabble nodded. 'Heh. I see.'

He let her lead him to the henburrow. Behind him, in Notratlan, he sensed the silence surge back. He heard the quiet movements of the few remaining Damplanders, the no-longer-nameless, as they moved off. He hoped they would run back to their clanlands, pour back down their runs and flood into their burrow. He hoped they would wash Rai'thir's poison away. He hoped that, finally, they could live like true rats. Ash had given them what they needed. Perhaps it was enough. Perhaps not. But none of it seemed to matter much. Not now Ash was gone.

Gabble walked past Ar'bus who lowered his head, and Snip who smiled sadly and placed a paw on his fur. Shrill stepped aside, still looking proudly away for his cat. And Gabble ducked beneath the wood, following Feather back up the passage, ready to tell the Mothers the story of their son.

Chapter fourteen

The Greenhedge formed a tangled black mass against the lightening sky. It loomed above them as Gabble and the Mothers trekked up the slope to the burrow. And inside, as Gabble followed them down the corridors, the daylight faded, leaving him in the enclosing dark of his once-home. Feather had gone ahead, to speak with her father, the Akla, and Gabble had promised to join her, once he had seen the Mothers safely home.

Together they made their way down through the broad chamber to the entrance to their burrow. The scents that greeted him were homely and familiar, but they brought little comfort. He would have given almost anything to go back in there, safely curled against Ash. But this was no longer his place. Ash was gone, and the Mothers' nests was for pups. Gabble

233

was not a pup any more. He wasn't a flapfoot or a ratling. He was a rat, with a true name that he kept in his heart next to his memory of Ash. Whisker and Bustle walked to the threshold then turned to face him, gently blocking the way. He saw his own grief reflected in their faces. For long moments the three rats merely stood and shared their unspoken loss. Then Whisker smiled. She stepped to Gabble, drew him into a hug and pressed her scent to his flank. She stepped back and gave him an odd look, sorrowful, yet proud.

'My Fo'dur,' she said. 'I always knew it was the right name for you.' She gave him a smile that twisted at its edge. 'You have truly earned it. You're a good rat.' Then she turned and left, disappearing down into her burrow. Fo'dur turned to Bustle. He wanted to say something, but words, finally, were not enough, not for a heart as full and empty as his. Instead he lowered his head. Bustle put her paws on his fur, and her whiskers tickled at his ear. She whispered a single word, and pressed her paws against him, with a smudge of her scent. Then she too turned, and followed Whisker.

Gabble stood, head bowed, for some moments, then moved away, making for the tunnels that led along the hedge. Here in the burrow-deep the darkness was absolute, but the sounds of the Greenhedge—all drowsy squabbles, rats pattering for their nests, the

cries of the young, and soft words from the Mothers—
were everywhere. And scents rose up from the earthen
floors, giving him a strange, warm chill of recognition.
They guided him down the old paths, telling him the
stories of the rats who had been here: here a Bigrat,
there a flapfoot, cheekily overscenting, a fight, sharp
in his nose, the old, the young, the Bigrats, and the
drudges. And this last scent was bitter. Drudges
were rats who scarcely dared to leave a mark, and if
they did it was timid, apologetic, resentful. But rats,
Gabble reminded himself, who, like the Damplanders'
nameless, had dreams. They too lived the best they
could, and he couldn't imagine that the Taker would
refuse them.

As Gabble walked the tunnels, the colony settled
around him, ready to rest for the day. His mind,
normally so crowded with thoughts, was oddly empty.
All he had was a single word, a name that Bustle had
given him. *Ra'lag.* Some of the names in Old Rat
were hard to understand. Over time their meanings
shifted and shaded until nobody could be sure what
they had first intended. This one could mean 'fearless',
or perhaps 'fear's end'. Gabble whispered it under his
breath, testing its shape with his lips. And as he spoke
the word into the burrow-quiet, he found a small smile
on his face. Ash's name. And, in the end, he too had
lived it well.

Feet approached from around a curve of the tunnel that led from the outside; a rat heading home. Gabble stepped aside to let him pass. The rat walked by, head up, scenting curiously. Heh. Gabble didn't smell right any more. He had been too many places the other rats hadn't. Too many rats had touched him, eroding the comfortable scents of home. He breathed a sigh, and kept his head down before continuing on his way. He had no need of trouble.

'Hey, you! Not so fast. Who are you?'

Gabble closed his eyes, and turned to face the rat. He breathed in its odour. The smell spoke of a rat who thought a lot of himself, but a decent sort who didn't want trouble. Gabble would have known the scent anywhere. After all, he had borne it in his name raid. He said, 'Because of you I name raided. And so I think I can tell you my true name. Heh. I'm Fo'dur,' he smiled, sadly. 'And you're Hector.'

'I don't know you, rat.' Hector sounded surprised. Gabble put his head on the side. Perhaps Hector really had forgotten him. After all, Gabble had been just another flapfoot when they name raided. Or perhaps he smelled so different that he truly no longer belonged.

'Heh. I'll remind you. My brother was a white rat. He and I raided as flapfeet. We went to Notratlan, found a henburrow, and raided an egg. We brought it home and earned our names.' Hector's breath hissed, but Gabble kept speaking. 'A strange name raid, heh? We ran with the Hunter that night, but I truly earned my name by dancing with the Trickster. And my brother earned his from the Taker himself.'

Hector blinked, then said, 'Ah. So that was you.' Gabble frowned as Hector continued, 'I've heard your story, just this night. Tales are spreading, Fo'dur, about your name and about your brother. The tale says that our Akla sent Bigrats to Notratlan to watch for Damplanders.' Hector's tone was serious. 'They saw a rat standing there, shouting that he was the Taker's Shining One, and calling himself by your name. They saw that rat taken by a cat, and carried away to the Land of Bones. They say he was punished for his insolence.' Hector sidled forwards, winkling his nose at the scent from Gabble's coat, and stopped, just beyond touching distance. He dropped his voice to a whisper. 'If I bore your name, Fo'dur, I would keep it to myself. There are already rats in the clan who think that your name is tainted by the Taker.'

Gabble stared at Hector. Is that what the clan thought? That his name was tainted? But yes. Of course, that's how the clan would see it. After everything that he had done, after Ash's sacrifice, after making sure the Damplanders would not come to Greenhedge, the rats here would believe the rumours and the easy half-truths. The full story was difficult, that a good rat had lost his way, but made amends and found his name right at the end. Nobody would believe that, not when they could think the worst. Gabble chuckled.

'Sorry, what's funny?' said Hector.

'Your story,' said Gabble. 'The clan. All of it. It's funny because it doesn't matter. Heh.' He shook his head. 'We all think we know about names, because the Akla grants them to us. But how many of us truly earn them in the raid? And how many live them after we have raided?'

Hector's brow furrowed. 'I don't understand.'

'No. Heh. But I'll tell you what I've learned from the oldest tale,' said Gabble, gently. 'We all carry a piece of the Mother's heart, and our name is a sign to the Taker that we are worthy to carry it. We hold it here,' he tapped his chest. 'We earn it by our actions and we keep the Mother's love pure. Names don't only come from the Hunter, and they're not earned only once. We earn them again and again, with every action and word.' He sighed. 'A name not lived is never really earned, I think. Don't rely on it. It'll be hollow, like old bones.'

Hector laughed, but the sound had an edge, as if he wasn't sure of himself. 'Maybe you're right,' said Hector after a pause. 'Thanks for the advice, and the story. Now I'd better return to my clan. I hope you can too.' He gave Gabble a sympathetic look. Then he left, being careful not to touch Gabble's fur.

Gabble stared after him, thinking hard. Then he too walked away, making for the Akla's chambers. And in the burrow chatter he now fancied that he caught the sound of his name, here and there, as a whispered story spread from mouth to mouth behind him: the tale of a white rat, once a flapfoot of the Greenhedge, who had defied the Taker and died with a tainted name.

Gabble came at last to the burrow of Ged'dur, the Akla, and he lingered outside. He remembered the last time he had been here, terrified of the Akla's size and his hard words. The scents emanating from inside were still as he remembered, but different, somehow. Now they seemed less impressive.

'What do you want, rat?' The Akla's words snapped out from the burrow.

'I want to talk with my Akla. If he still is.'

A pause, and then, 'Yes. I've been waiting for you. Come, then.'

Gabble stepped into the Akla's chambers.

'I've been speaking with my daughter,' said the Akla, looking up at Gabble. 'She gave me your message, about the Damplanders at Notratlan. I sent your Mothers as you asked, and I readied the clan.'

'It's good that you did,' said Gabble. 'If it hadn't been for Ash the Damplanders would have taken the henburrow.'

'If it hadn't been for Ash,' Ged'dur snapped, 'the Damplanders would never have dared. It was he who went to them. And you too.' He glared. 'You defied me, Gabble. You returned to Notratlan. You took my daughter to the Damplanders. I gave you your name, and that was how you chose to repay me.'

'My name is Fo'dur,' said Gabble, quietly, 'and I earned it for myself. And yes, I did both, for the love of a brother, and the good of the clan.' He stepped forwards, closer to the Akla. 'But I never had anything to repay for my name. I see things differently now. You owe *me* a debt, I think.'

'I warn you—' Ged'dur began, but Gabble overrode him.

'Who told Ash about the eggs in Notratlan? Somebody did.'

Ged'dur's snarl turned to surprise, with a flicker of recognition. The expression was gone almost immediately, replaced by a cool, bland look. But Gabble had been watching closely, and he knew he had it right.

'So it *was* you. Heh. That's why Ash wanted to name raid there. And you made sure of it.'

'Gabble—' the Akla began.

'Use my true name,' said Gabble. 'You owe me that at least.' And now a quiet rage bubbled through his thoughts. 'You did it because Ash was different. Because his mouth was too big and he caused too much trouble. He disrupted your clan, didn't he?' Ged'dur did not speak, but waited and listened. 'So you let him know about Notratlan. You sent a flapfoot there, knowing that he might not come back, because he was strange, because he looked different. Because he'd come back humbled or he wouldn't come back. And either way the clan would win, right?' Gabble was almost shaking with anger. 'You told me that the Akla seeks the clan's best interests. Is this how you treat the clan?'

'Yes,' replied Ged'dur calmly. 'It is. Notratlan serves a purpose. The Bigrats know of it, and sometimes they pass that knowledge on, when they think it's necessary.' He frowned. 'The clan needs to be afraid of Notratlan. It keeps us together and away from the Damplanders. Fo'dur, I told you that the clan is the cradle that holds us. And it's delicate. We didn't *send* your brother anywhere. We let him know about the eggs, and that he was forbidden to go there. The same way that, as a flapfoot, he was forbidden to name raid. And, yes, we did that knowing that he would go anyway.' Ged'dur held Gabble's gaze. 'You have to understand that rats like your brother are dangerous. They do anything they want, without thinking, and without a care. They bring danger. If your brother had not been hurt in Notratlan he would have gone further, done more harm. As it was he went to the Damplanders and led them to

241

Notratlan. Rats like him are marked by the Taker. And there's no place for them in a clan.'

Gabble shook his head. He did not want to believe the Akla would do this. But he knew that Ged'dur spoke the truth. 'You put Ash in danger. And because of you he got ill and went to the Damplanders. And when I followed him you sent Feather to watch me, to make sure I wasn't going against you. And I did everything I could to save him, and the clan.' Gabble took a breath. 'So I say you owe me. You owe me a debt for the suffering of my brother, and the paths I have danced and the truths I have twisted to save him. You owe me for my Mothers' tears. You owe me a debt. And so does the Greenhedge.'

Ged'dur's eyes narrowed as he considered Fo'dur's words. 'Perhaps it is as you say, Fo'dur. And if the clan owes you a debt, what then? What would you ask of it?'

'I want to know if there's a place here for a rat like me.'

And now, for the first time, Ged'dur looked uncomfortable. He turned away. 'The clan will decide for itself whether you belong,' he said. 'That's not for me to say.' He moved aside with a shake of his head. And now, somehow, he seemed less like an Akla, and more like a normal rat. He was huge, scarred, and strong, but also careworn. 'Fo'dur, I can't tell the clan what to do, or what to think. All I do is try to keep it working. And sometimes that means that good rats must suffer. Sometimes that means hearing a tale that I know to be untrue spoken in the voices of every clanrat, and keeping silent. If that tale is of a name then you can be sure that it will spread and rats will believe it. And this choice, like all of the others, I must live with.' Ged'dur's nose twitched and he pulled a face. 'You smell of the Damplanders. For that reason among many the clan may not welcome you back. Rats talk, Fo'dur. Already they know about the white rat who took your name to the Damplands.'

Then Ged'dur sighed. He took two steps forward and pressed his paws to Gabble's flanks, leaving his scent.

'There,' he said. 'The Akla's mark. His approval. His thanks for everything you did and acknowledgement of everything you lost. Perhaps the others will smell it on you and take you back. But more probably they won't. Either way, this is all I can do. I'm only one rat.' He smiled and opened his paws. 'The confession of an Akla. For what's it's worth, I'm grateful to you. You returned my daughter to me, and you fought for the clan. And I'm sorry any of this happened, I really am.'

'Yes,' said Gabble. 'So am I.'

As Gabble turned to leave Ged'dur muttered something beneath his breath. Then he raised his voice.

'I know I will regret this,' he said, 'but a rat should repay his debts, even though this one, I think, will cost me dear.' Gabble turned to him, puzzled. The Akla faced him, unsmiling. 'Listen carefully, Fo'dur. I did not ask Feather to follow you. She went of her own accord, despite everything I said to stop her. That is the truth, and you can make of it what you will.'

Then the Akla settled back against the wall and closed his eyes. 'I have given you everything I can. And now, I think, it is time for you to go.'

Reddish light illuminated the burrow entrance, but left the tunnel behind in darkness. At the edge of hearing were the scrabbles and cries and constant rat-babble of a thriving burrow, readying itself for the night. But here, at the edge of Gabble's home, these were almost drowned by the sounds of the world beyond. Birds called, leaves rustled, and the wind stirred the grasses. And Gabble, standing alone, was filled with emptiness. A few ratlings shoved past, excited to be heading out. He watched enviously as they disappeared into the night. The Hunter willing, they would be coming back to their nests, with paws full of prizes and their voices full of their deeds. The wind picked up, bringing up a wealth of scents from the runs, but also, beyond that, from the earth, the plants and the myriad small things of the world. He filled his thoughts with them, enjoying the breeze in his whiskers, and tried to forget his home. The smells from the burrow behind him, once so familiar, had taken on a bitter note. They were the same as ever they had been, but now they *felt* wrong. Not hostile, exactly, but tense. Gabble let go his breath. Tonight or tomorrow night, what difference would it make?

Something approached down the tunnel behind him, and arrived with a surge of scent and a whirl of hair. Gabble closed his eyes. This was going to hurt. But still he was glad she was here.

'Where have you been?' Feather demanded. 'I've been looking for you everywhere.'

Gabble did not reply. His throat had gone tight, as though too many words had jammed in it. Instead he inclined his head and remained silent.

'Oh, that's nice,' she snapped. 'You could at least answer me.' She shoved past him out of the burrow and turned to face him, scowling. But when she saw his expression she raised a paw. 'Um, is everything all right?'

'Yes,' Gabble managed, looking away. And then, 'No. I'm sorry.'

Feather stepped closer, nose twitching. She sniffed at Gabble's flank and then put a paw on his shoulder, turning him to face her.

'They're not marking you, are they?'

Gabble shook his head. 'No. The Akla tried, but the

clan doesn't want me. They say my name is tainted, that I'm touched by the Taker. And so they won't touch me.' He chuckled. 'Funny, really.'

'Funny?'

'Not the right word. But we saved the clan from the Damplanders, and now they're scared that I am one.' A smile played across Gabble's lips. 'Well, they're right about one thing. I was never really a Hunter. And soon I'll be a Trickster with no home.'

'So what do we do?'

'We?' Gabble murmured. 'Feather, *we* don't do anything. You're the Akla's daughter. You will be clan Mother, and you—'

'I'm nothing I don't want to be,' said Feather. 'And nobody tells me what to do. Right?'

Gabble smiled at her. 'Right. Heh. Not unless they want thumping.'

Feather looked a bit abashed, but then she raised her chin. 'Exactly,' she said. And then she smiled. Gabble found himself grinning back at her. With rats like Feather around, the world wasn't so bad.

'I want to say sorry,' said Gabble. 'When you came to Notratlan, I thought your father had sent you. But he told me that he hadn't.'

Feather nodded. 'That's right, he hadn't.'

'Heh. So that explains one of the times you hit me. But why *did* you follow me?'

Feather stared off down the slope. Then she swallowed and met Gabble's gaze.

'Because I liked you,' she said, finally. 'You seemed nice. You talked to me, you know, like I was a normal rat.' She took a hesitant step closer. Gabble barely dared move. 'So I chose to follow you. I thought you might need my help. And . . . and I'd like to keep helping you.' Feather put her head on one side. 'If you'll have me.'

Gabble's mouth dropped open. 'I can't ask you to do that. Feather, I have to leave the clan.'

'Yes,' said Feather, 'I know. Stop treating me like I'm stupid.'

Gabble swallowed. His eyes met hers and the oddest feeling stole over him. He had been ready to leave it all behind. But now . . . now, perhaps, he wouldn't have to. Not entirely. One of the most important parts of the clan was here, standing right next to him. And she had been all along. He had been so caught up in trying to help Ash that he had barely noticed, but now he remembered Feather's paws, helping him, holding him, cradling him against the hurt. And he realized, right when it was almost too late, that he owed her more than anyone else. And even if she didn't feel the debt, he knew that he wanted to pay it anyway. *A clan is the cradle that holds us*, he thought. *Well, maybe a clan could be just two rats.*

'But I'm such a stupid rat,' said Gabble. 'I've given you nothing.'

'I wasn't asking for anything,' said Feather, gently. 'Not until now.'

Gabble nodded, then raised his eyes. 'I don't know where we'll go. Maybe to Ar'bus, if he'll take us in. Maybe it'll have to be further.' He smiled. 'I saw something, once, down in the Damplands, like a ribbon of water. It was beautiful. Maybe I could show it to you.'

Feather broke into a broad grin. But then she caught his eye and straightened. 'That's decided then,' she said, trying to sound matter-of-fact. 'Good. You need looking after.' She gave him a shy smile. 'And it'll be nice to run with you, Gabble.'

'Gabble. Heh. I don't think I feel like a Gabble any more.'

'No? Why not?'

'Maybe I've gabbled enough for a while. Maybe it's time to change. That's all.' He smiled. 'I'm Fo'dur. Heh.'

'Yes. I was there.' Feather gave him a searching look. 'All right. Fo'dur it is, then.' She nodded, fitting his name to his face. 'It suits you. I'm Car'ma.'

Fo'dur's brow furrowed, trying to translate from the Old Rat. He gave her a sidelong look. 'That means "Trouble".'

Car'ma squeaked indignantly. 'No, it doesn't. And 'Fo'dur' sounds like a considerate, lovable rat. You'd better start acting it if that's what you want to be called.' But she pressed closer to him, and together they watched the blackness creep amongst the roots and branches of the hedge.

'How long do we have?' said Car'ma. 'You know, before we leave?'

'Heh. Not long. Tonight or tomorrow.'

Car'ma stretched out her limbs and her tail whisked from side to side. She cocked her head, her eyes bright. 'That makes life easy, then,' she said. 'It's going to be a cloudy night. Good for trips to Notratlan.'

And before Fo'dur could speak, she gave him a thump on the shoulder and was twisting her way down the slope to the main run. She stopped at the bottom, waiting for him. Fo'dur glanced back at the hedge. So they were going, then. Funny. It didn't feel nearly as terrible as it could have done. Just one step, then another, and he was beyond the clan forever. But now he was running with a rat called Car'ma who wanted to stay with him. He held the thought in his heart, in the place where he kept his name, and his memory of Ash. He pattered down the slope to join her and they ran on together. A small, fierce happiness grew in Fo'dur. *Car'ma*, he thought. It meant 'my own way'. He stole a look over at her, thinking that life now would be easier to face. But then she caught him looking.

'Watch where you're going,' she said, and barged deliberately into him. He nearly fell, and when he had staggered back to his feet she had pulled ahead. He had to sprint to catch up, making his still-aching body protest. *My own way. Heh.* Life might be easier with her by his side, he thought, but only if that was what she chose to make it.

A note from the author

Trickster, if you hadn't noticed, is a story about rats. (I'm not sure how you wouldn't have noticed, but if you didn't then one of us went wrong. It was probably me.) To write it I had to learn a lot, and was lucky to be able to phone a friend. Manuel Berdoy is a rat expert and all round star. He answered some truly stupid questions and pointed me in the right direction. He has also written and directed *The Laboratory Rat: A Natural History*, a wonderful film about rat behaviour that you can still find online (but do ask your parents first). Another brilliant online source I regularly visited was Anne's Rat Page (by Anne Hanson), which answers almost any question you could imagine about how rats see the world—but be warned, there's lots of detail.

If you find any clips of rats and watch them, you will see rats behaving just as Gabble and Ash do. But you might also spot places in *Trickster* where the characters do things that real rats wouldn't. If you noticed any, then really well done—but remember that stories have lives and rules of their own (they're selfish beasts, stories, and always want things their way).

Anyway, thank you so much for reading. I hope you enjoyed my rats' tale!

Tom

Tom Moorhouse lives in Oxford. When not writing fiction he works as an ecologist at Oxford University's Zoology Department. Over the years he has met quite a lot of wildlife. Most of it tried to bite him. He loves hiking up mountains, walking through woods, climbing on rocks, and generally being weather-beaten outdoors.

Other books by Tom Moorhouse.

Something was approaching the burrow. Something deadly. Something that made Sylvan's fur bristle with fear . . .

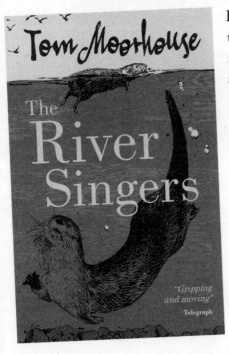

Knowing their lives are under threat, Sylvan and his brother and sisters have no choice but to abandon their burrow for ever. Together they set out on an epic journey along the Great River; but with dangers lurking at every turn, will they ever find a safe place to call home?

Adventure is just a whisker away . . .

Kale and Strife are two young water voles with a nose for trouble and an eye for adventure. But when their uncle Sylvan comes to stay, bringing news of a terrible danger that could threaten their whole existence, the voles are sucked into a quest that will test their courage and friendship to the limit.

Tom Moorhouse

The Rising

'Does for the vole what BABE author Dick King-Smith did for the pig...'

The Times

Ready for more stories...

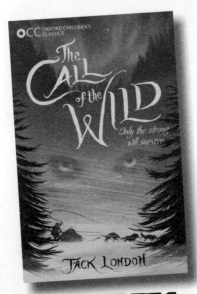

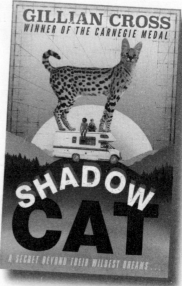